Taking
Control

a Babysitting a Billionaire novel

Nina Croft

Entangled Publishing, LLC
2614 South Timberline Road
Suite 109
Fort Collins, CO 80525
Visit our website at www.entangledpublishing.com.

Brazen is an imprint of Entangled Publishing, LLC. For more information on our titles, visit www.brazenbooks.com.

Edited by Candace Havens and Allison Collins
Cover design by Heather Howland
Photography by iStock

Manufactured in the United States of America

First Edition December 2014

For Rob…my hero!

Chapter One

Declan climbed out of his BMW sedan and handed the keys to the security guard. As he strolled toward the double glass doors of McCabe Industries, the now familiar sense of suffocation slowed his pace, and he had to fight the urge to turn around and run.

Christ, he was twenty-nine. Running away was hardly an option. Besides, where the hell would he run to? This was his life, and it was fucking perfect. He'd achieved everything he'd set out to. And yet each day it became harder to pretend he gave a shit.

He caught a reflection of himself in the glass doors. Dark suit, dark blue tie—like a million other businessmen—and the sense of suffocation tightened around him. As he forced it down, a loud *crack* rose above the rumble of traffic behind him, and the image shattered into a thousand pieces.

A second *crack* and some inner sense made him jerk to the side as something punched into him, whirling him around.

He crashed to the concrete, his head hitting the curb, and everything went black.

When he came to, he was lying on his back, the smell of antiseptic thick in the air. He opened his eyes and stared at the white ceiling. He was pretty sure he was in a hospital bed, his brain was thumping, and his right arm was on fire. "Crap."

"Welcome back."

He rolled his head, blinked to clear his vision, and found his father standing beside him.

"What happened?" he asked.

"Someone shot you. And no prizes for guessing who or why."

His dad sounded pissed. Hardly surprising. Being shot was not a respectable pastime for a CEO.

Declan pushed himself up, flinching as pain raced from his shoulder to his wrist. He was still wearing his pants, but his chest was bare and a white bandage wrapped around his upper arm, blood already staining the cloth. "How bad is it? I have a meeting this afternoon."

"You've just been fucking shot. Forget about the fucking meeting." More than pissed. Worried. He hadn't seen his dad this worried since Declan had nearly gone off the rails and fallen in love ten years ago.

"It's an important meeting."

"No. You're the only thing that's important right now. Jesus, you could have died."

It was true. Declan waited for some reaction to that— fear, anger…but his mind remained numb. "Has news of the shooting gotten out? Has it affected the share price?"

"Will you stop thinking about the goddamn business?

The goddamn business doesn't matter."

Declan raised an eyebrow. "You brought me up to think the business is the *only* thing that matters."

"Well, maybe I was wrong."

His eyes narrowed on his father. "Have they given me drugs? Am I hallucinating?"

"Ha-ha." He shrugged. "But there's more to life...shit. Let's not go into this now. We'll talk later. When you're better."

Declan opened his mouth to say *How about never?* They didn't have those sorts of conversations, but the doctor came in at that moment and the next minutes were taken up with medical stuff.

His father had been acting strange since Declan had returned to the UK eleven months ago. This wasn't the first time he'd suggested that the business wasn't everything. Since when? His dad had even been trying his hand at matchmaking, pushing everything from corporate lawyers to exotic dancers under Declan's nose. It was surreal, and it was driving him crazy.

"How bad is it?" he asked the doctor as the bandage came off.

"Not bad, considering. The bullet went right through. I'm going to give you some stitches. Otherwise you have a bang on the head, and we'll keep you in overnight in case there's any concussion."

"I have a—"

"He'll stay," his dad interrupted. "If I have to tie him to the goddamned bed."

His father really was upset. Which was weird. Rory McCabe did not do upset. "I've arranged for Pete to stay here tonight," he said, a frown turning down the corners of his mouth. "He'll stand guard outside your room. Then tomorrow, we'll get you some bodyguards."

"You're joking, aren't you?"

"Do I look like I'm fucking joking?"

Declan glanced away from the doctor stitching the wound to where his father leaned against the wall arms folded across his chest. No, he didn't; he looked deadly serious. "I don't need a minder, dad."

"You're sitting in ER having a bullet wound stitched up. I say that pretty much means you do."

He did have a point, but somehow, Declan couldn't get worked up about it. "I knew the risks when I went to the police."

"And I warned you against it."

"Why? Were they old mates of yours?"

For a moment, his father's expression tightened, and then he grinned. "More likely old enemies. Let's just say that I know the type."

Yeah, his old dad would know the type. McCabe Industries was now totally legitimate, but it hadn't always been that way. His father's wealth had been built on illegal gambling, smuggling, and prostitution. That was all behind him now, but Declan was betting he still had a few dodgy contacts.

"And they will want to make an example of you," his dad continued. "I'm doing what I can, calling in some old debts, but until I clear this up, I want to make sure you're safe."

"And you intend to do that by getting me some goddamned babysitters?"

"I'll get in touch with some security firms, find out who's the best at this sort of thing, and hire you some protection."

Six months ago, Declan had come across evidence that one of his subsidiary companies was being used to launder money by a drug cartel. He'd gone to the police, and he'd been working with them since to uncover the assholes behind it. Now they'd succeeded, and those assholes were unhappy with Declan. They wanted revenge and to make an example of him, preferably before the case came to trial in three weeks' time.

And this morning, he'd been shot.

That didn't mean he had to have some crappy bodyguards shadowing his every movement. He glanced over to where his father still leaned against the wall. "I don't need a bodyguard. I'll be careful."

"You'll have them, or I'll tell your mother about this."

God forbid. He obviously meant business. Declan couldn't remember the last time his father and mother had even spoken. Maybe his sister's wedding five years ago? Even then, he suspected they'd managed to get through the proceedings without talking. Strangely, they had never divorced, but they also did their bests to never meet. As they lived on different sides of the Atlantic Ocean, it wasn't difficult. Declan knew all about the effectiveness of putting an ocean between you and someone you didn't want to encounter.

He gritted his teeth as the doctor made the final stitch, then released his breath. He wasn't a baby. And he didn't need babysitting. But maybe it wasn't worth arguing with his dad about the matter. He'd see these security people, pay their retainer, and then tell them to keep the hell away from him.

He had a business to run.

...

Somewhere along the way, Jessica Bauer had lost the ability—and if she was honest, the inclination—to play nice. While it had started out as a cross between payback and a defense mechanism, now it was second nature. She was the first to admit it; she was a badass with attitude issues.

But that didn't mean she couldn't change; she was trying. Her biggest problem with that was she liked being a badass. It beat the crap out of being a pathetic wimp with a broken heart.

She drummed her fingers on the tabletop as she contemplated the man sitting across from her. Phil ticked all the right boxes. A few years older than her, handsome in a blond, bland sort of way, and dressed in a dark blue suit, he looked what he was: a successful city accountant. A *nice* man. In fact, just what she'd asked for.

And she was bored out of her mind.

She took a large slug of red wine, hoping to numb her senses. Just a little while longer and she could go. Cross Phil off the list. He was her third offering from the dating agency and going just about as well as the first two. She was out of practice that was all. She'd get better.

"Tell me about yourself, Jessica," Phil said when she remained silent. "What do you like to do in your spare time?"

She opened her mouth to answer that she liked shooting guns and beating people up, when she was saved by the muted buzz of her cell phone. Caller ID showed it was her boss, Jake. Reprieve. Sometimes she just loved him.

Or she would if he'd give her the promotion she deserved.

"I know it's your day off," Jake said, "but we've had an emergency request and—"

"I'm on my way." She slipped the phone back in her pocket and faced the man opposite her. "Sorry, Phil. But duty calls."

"Oh." She'd thought his smile was a permanent fixture; now it faded. "You want to meet again?" he asked.

She reached across and patted his hand. "I'll give you a call." *Or not.*

"Hey, what's happening?" she asked as she strolled into Jake's office ten minutes later. He was lounging in his big chair, behind his big desk. Soon to be hers.

One of the toughest guys she had ever met, these days Jake had the look of a sleepy, sated tiger. But then he was a newlywed, married to Jess's best friend, Kim.

Recently, he'd decided he wanted to spend more time with his pregnant wife and was pulling back from some of the businesses, including stepping down as CEO of Knight Securities, one of the premier security firms in London. Jess had been his second in command for two years and worked for the company for the last five, ever since they'd both left the army. She was the obvious choice for the job, but Jake was balking at making the final decision.

She wanted this job. She deserved this job.

But the desk would have to go. Ever since Kim had told her that she and Jake had shagged on top of that particular piece of furniture, she'd never been able to look at it the same way. Now she shook her head to dispel the disturbing mental image.

"Is there a problem?" Jake asked.

"Just wondering if I should order myself a new desk. I know what's happened on top of that one and I'm not sure I want it in my office."

"Not your office yet." He sat forward and gave her a long, hard look. The sort of look that would have made her squirm…had she been the squirmy type. "And if the report I got from the Jennings job is anything to go by, it never will be."

Bloody hell. She should have known Gary would tattle. He was the other person in the running for the CEO position. "Jennings is an asshole."

"Perhaps. But did you really have to tell him that?"

"It seemed like a good idea at the time." Along with informing him that if he touched her ass one more time she'd shoot him herself. Life was too short to take that sort of crap.

Jake studied her for what seemed an age, and she held herself very still. "Sit down, Jess."

She sat.

"You do know that a big part of my job is keeping the clients happy?" he said.

She stiffened her spine and sat up straighter in the chair. This conversation wasn't heading anywhere good. "Yes."

"Well, the problem is, I'm not even sure we'll have any clients left if I put you in charge. Jennings isn't the first you've upset. You're too…confrontational."

"I haven't called anyone else an asshole." Well, not for a while anyway.

Jake ignored the interruption. "I've known you a long time, and you've always been the same—hard as nails and pretty screwed up as far as men are concerned. It hasn't mattered, and it was none of my business. It matters now."

That was bad news. "It does?"

"Yes. If you're serious about wanting this job. Whatever happened to you in the past, you need to get over it. Let it go and move on." He sat back. "Okay, lecture over, but you get one more chance—upset this client and you'll make Gary a very happy man."

She glared. "You wouldn't."

"Just watch me. I'd rather not. Apart from the PR stuff, you're better than he is, but I will if you don't learn to think before you open your mouth."

She wanted to argue, but deep down she knew he was right. Actually, not that deep down. But she'd always relished a challenge...being "nice" was just another. Taking a deep breath, she curved her lips into a bright smile. "I can do that. In fact, I'll make you a deal: if I don't have this next client eating out of my hand and singing my praises, then you're welcome to give the job to Gary."

Jake snorted.

She ignored him. "So what is this emergency job? Who's the client?"

"Bodyguard. CEO of one of the big multinationals."

"But why call me in? Both Dave and Steve are free since the job they were on was canceled. They're doing surveillance but bored out of their minds."

"Because the client asked for you."

"Oh." She wasn't usually requested for bodyguard work, at least not for men. Most didn't believe a woman could protect them. "Let me see."

Jake swiveled the screen so she could read the report.

For a second, the words blurred, as though her brain didn't want to register the information.

Maybe she was hallucinating. Jake's orders to put the past behind her had obviously had the opposite effect and conjured up the name in front of her. She blinked, then again, but the letters refused to realign into something more acceptable.

Could it be a different Declan McCabe? Unlikely.

"Sorry. I can't do it."

Jake's brows drew together. "You can't? I thought you'd jump at the chance."

She gave what she hoped was a casual shrug. "I'm tied up with a few other jobs right now."

"So reallocate them. I have an overwhelming urge to see this client eating out of your hand. I looked him up and he's got a reputation as a ruthless bastard."

She swallowed. "He does?"

"Yeah. Cold as ice. I'll tell you what. I'll make *you* a deal—you keep him sweet, prove you can do it, and my job is yours."

Well, that wasn't good news. What chance was there of her keeping Declan McCabe sweet? None, she was betting. "So why does he need a bodyguard?"

"Someone shot him this morning."

An unwelcome jolt of shock stabbed her in the solar plexus. "Is he all right?"

"They just winged him."

She let out her breath in a sigh. Though why she should worry about the asshole bastard who had broken her heart she didn't know. For many years, she would have gladly put a bullet into him herself. Or if she'd ever thought about him she would have. Which she didn't. Because she hated him.

Then something else triggered. "You said he asked for me?"

"Yes."

"Specifically by name?"

"Yes." A frown was forming between Jake's brows. "You know this man?"

"No," she said quickly. Too quickly, and Jake's frown deepened. She swallowed, then took a deep breath, wiped her palms down her thighs. She had to get out of there, get herself under control before she gave herself away. "I'll go see if I can reallocate those jobs." Without waiting for him to answer, she pushed herself up and headed for the door.

"Are you okay?"

Jake's words halted her as she reached for the handle. She didn't turn. "Why wouldn't I be?" And she was out of there.

Her mind hammered against her skull. Declan had asked for her. Why? And who'd shot him? His father had owned nightclubs and been into all sorts of dubious stuff. Maybe Declan had gone the same way. Though she doubted that. He'd always been a sanctimonious prick.

And he'd asked for her.

Bugger.

She needed to hit something. Jake had installed a gym in the basement of the building and she headed down there. Just beat up the punching bag and get it out of her system. Even better, she met one of the other operatives on her way down in the elevator.

"You going for a workout?" she asked.

"Yeah," he said eyeing her dubiously.

She guessed she looked a little tense. "Good. I feel like beating the crap out of something. I was going to use the punching bag, but I'm guessing you'll be much more satisfying." Steve was six foot four and three years younger than her.

Half an hour later and she was breathing hard, but not as hard as Steve. He leaned against the wall, wiping the sweat from his forehead with the back of his hand.

"Does this mean you like me?" he asked. "You wouldn't beat up on me if you didn't like me, right?"

"Wrong."

"Come on, Jess. Admit it. Come out for a drink with me tonight."

"I don't shit on my own doorstep." Actually, she didn't shit on anyone's doorstep, but that was none of Steve's business. "Besides, I'm betting you only asked because you want to win the wager."

She was quite aware the guys had a pool going on who could actually get her on a date. She could have told them to save their energy. Actually, she had told them, numerous times. It was never going to happen. While she was willing to go through with this whole looking-for-a-man thing, she wanted a nice man. Not one of the screwed-up adrenaline junkies who worked here.

"Maybe," Steve said. "But we'd be good together."

"No, we wouldn't." She was going to find herself an accountant or a lawyer.

"You don't like men very much, do you?"

She curled the corner of her lip. "What's there to like?" Okay, so that hadn't been nice. *Must try harder.*

"Your loss, but I hate to see such a beautiful woman end up dried up and alone." He shrugged, but headed back to the changing rooms, leaving her with less than pleasant thoughts.

She leaned back against the wall and slid down until she sat on the floor, hugging her knees. She'd always thought Steve a bit thick, but he was spot-on with this one. Dried up and alone.

But she could change. She was trying. Christ, she'd even joined a dating agency. It wasn't her fault all the men she had met so far had bored the pants off her. Well, actually, it was her fault; she had filled out the form for the dating agency after all. And she might as well have put "boring" on the necessary criteria. She made a mental note to tweak the form.

Plus, she was the first to admit she had unresolved issues.

Jake's words came back to her. Could she let the past go? An image of Declan flashed up in her mind, all dark tousled hair and boyish good looks. Perhaps this was fate, and if she saw Declan after all these years, she'd no doubt find he was no different than any other man, just a boring businessman like Phil. And finally, she could cut the hatred from her mind, cauterize the wound, and start over, move on. After all, it hadn't been *all* Declan's fault. She had to take some of the blame. A tiny, tiny little bit of it.

She pushed herself up and headed back to the changing rooms, pulled her phone from her bag, and hit Jake's internal number before she could change her mind.

"The McCabe job. Set up a meeting for tomorrow."

She ended the call before she could think any more. Thinking would not be good right now.

Thinking would probably make her realize that this was a really bad idea.

Chapter Two

Something sharp stabbed repeatedly at the inside of his skull. Declan rested his head against the back of his chair, closed his eyes, and tried to ignore the pain.

So far, he'd resisted taking any medication, wanting to keep his mind sharp, but now he pulled the small bottle of painkillers out of his pocket and swallowed two, washing them down with a gulp of water.

Within minutes, he felt the effect, even the burn in his upper arm fading to numbness.

But at least when he hurt he was feeling something.

He hadn't lived in London for over ten years, since the summer before he'd started Harvard. He'd thought the move back here might have eased his restlessness, but if anything it had increased.

The boredom was what had led to the shooting in the first place. He could have kept out of the whole money-laundering thing, just handed the information to the police and he wouldn't be sitting here now with a bullet hole in his arm, waiting to have a meeting with a bunch of bodyguards he didn't want or need.

He'd only agreed to this meeting because it was easier to get rid of the bodyguards than get rid of his father. No doubt he would hear from him soon enough, but he would deal with that then.

The intercom on his desk buzzed, and he pressed it.

"Your ten o'clock meeting is here," Paul, his assistant, said.

"Send them in."

He'd stayed the night in the hospital, but discharged himself first thing this morning. Now he had work to catch up on, and he meant to deal with this as quickly as possible.

Then the door opened and for a moment, his world stopped.

The strength drained from him, and the room went dim. He slumped back against his chair.

"Declan," Paul said. "Are you okay?"

He blinked, shook his head. "Of course I'm okay."

His assistant frowned, but stepped to the side. "These are the people from Knight Security. Ms. Bauer and Mr. Grantham."

He ignored the man, his gaze fixed on the woman who stood slightly to the front.

What the hell was she doing here?

Maybe he was hallucinating. His mind felt sluggish, and he wished he hadn't taken the pills. Except, he couldn't re-ally blame the painkillers. He was in shock. She was the last person he had expected to come through that door.

Around five foot ten, she was tall for a woman, still mod-el-slim in the black pantsuit. Beneath it, she wore a white button-down shirt and beneath that, he could make out the shape of her full breasts. He looked away quickly and up into her face.

He wasn't sure what he was expecting, a shock to match his own maybe, but her face was blank of expression. Of course, she would have known who she was coming to see. She would have prepared for this meeting. Would have had time to get the shock under control.

Either that or she'd forgotten him totally. It had been over ten years.

She was still the most beautiful woman he had ever seen. Her platinum fall of hair was pulled back into a ponytail, revealing the perfect oval of her face, with its high cheekbones, midnight-blue eyes under arched brows, and her full mouth. God, he'd loved her mouth, the things she'd done with those lips…

And shit, he shouldn't be thinking about those lips. But it was too late; the blood had shot straight to his dick, and he shifted in his chair.

Then his eyes settled on the scar, a pale line that ran from just below her right eye over her cheek to the corner of her mouth. It pulled her upper lip slightly, giving her what looked like a permanent sneer. She hadn't even attempted to hide it with makeup. In fact, now he looked, she wasn't wearing any makeup at all. Not even lipstick on her pink, full lips. But the scar didn't detract from her looks; rather it emphasized the perfection of the rest of her.

She was gazing at him out of those blue eyes with no hint of recognition, and he gritted his teeth. What the hell right did she have to forget him? Once she'd told him she'd love him forever. Of course, that was before he'd walked out on her, but all the same…

"Declan?" It was Paul again, dragging him from his less

than happy thoughts. His assistant appeared a little uncertain, probably wasn't used to his boss behaving in such a shell-shocked manner.

"I'm fine," he said. He had inherited Paul from his father, who'd taken him on as part of an old debt—the details of which Declan was sure he was better off not knowing. And it wouldn't surprise him if his assistant still reported back to his old boss. Declan hadn't cared enough to check out the man's loyalties, but he didn't want Paul reporting to his dad that he was unwell. He'd probably have to deal with a nurse as well as a bodyguard. He picked up the pill bottle from the desk and shook it. "Painkillers just kicking in," he said and Paul nodded.

Rising to his feet, Declan fastened his jacket to hide the fact that he was already hard just from looking at her. "That will be all," he said.

After his assistant had left the room, closing the door behind him, Declan gestured to the seats in front of his desk.

Her colleague came forward first, casting a sideways glance at Jess as he passed her as though she wasn't behaving quite as expected. Maybe she wasn't quite as composed as she appeared.

He studied the man briefly. He was big, but from the fluid way he moved, Declan reckoned the bulk was all muscle. He looked ex-army, his sandy hair cut military short.

"Mr. McCabe," he said, coming to a halt in front of the desk and extending his hand. Declan took it then winced as pain shot through his arm.

"Sorry," Grantham said. "I hear you took a bullet yesterday, must be painful."

"A scratch, nothing more."

The man sat and Declan turned his attention back to Jess. She still stood just inside the doorway. As she caught his glance, she shook herself and took a few steps forward. Unlike her male comrade though, she didn't hold her hand out for him to take, just sat in the seat and stared straight ahead. Her skin was pale, almost white, and a pulse beat in her throat. Definitely not as composed as she appeared, or wanted to appear.

Good.

He took his own seat, sat back, and pulled his shattered thoughts together. He'd planned to tell them they were not needed, and this changed nothing. They still weren't needed. He had no use for a bodyguard, and he certainly had no wish for Jess to jump in front of a bullet for him. Anyway, she'd probably be more likely to shoot him herself.

"I'm afraid your journey has been wasted. I won't be needing your services. I will of course pay for your time." He watched her closely as he spoke, not quite sure what response he expected or even wanted. Maybe it was better that she had forgotten him. If she had.

Of course, there was always the chance that she was just acting. Maybe she recognized him—how the fuck could she not?—but she wanted to avoid rehashing old times.

The man beside her frowned. "Has the…situation been resolved? I was under the impression we were needed until the court case."

"No, but I don't require a bodyguard," Declan said. "I'll take precautions. I can look after myself."

Jess snorted. He turned his attention to her as she raised one arched brow. "Well, you're certainly doing a good job so far. And could you not have phoned up and canceled the meeting, Mr. McCabe?" Her tone was cool, bordering on insolent. "As a professional courtesy. Or don't you think the people you employ deserve courtesy?"

"I promised my father I would see you, and I have."

For the first time, shock flashed across her features, her eyes narrowing, a frown forming between her brows. She was astonishingly beautiful, he'd forgotten just how stunning she was—well not so much forgotten as pushed the knowledge from his mind. Now his brain flooded with memories of her, dancing, her hair wild about her face, drinking shots, daring him to match her, lying beneath him, her eyes almost black with passion as she fell apart for him. Shit. He needed to stop thinking like this. He needed to get his head together.

But however much he would like to deny it, a deep, slow burn of excitement was starting low down in his belly. He wanted to push her, make her acknowledge him, but maybe not just yet. First, he needed to pull himself together. Whatever happened next, he planned to be in control of it.

"Your *father* arranged this?" Jess said, and he could hear the disbelief in her voice and something else.

He gave a bland smile. "He worries about me. He has my best interests at heart."

"I bet he does," she muttered, and this time her comrade did turn to look at her.

"Do we have a problem here, Jess?"

Declan shot a glance at the other man. He didn't like the familiar way he addressed Jessica. They obviously knew each other well. How well?

"Of course we don't have a problem," Jess said. Her tone should have been conciliatory instead, it was…sarcastic. "Mr. McCabe is the one with the problem," she continued.

"Someone wants him dead, but I'm sure that's not a first. Probably lots of people have wanted Mr. McCabe dead. But as he said, he's a big boy, and he can look after himself. And if not, I'm sure his daddy can do it for him."

God, she was a bitch. He liked it.

Her colleague obviously gave up at that point. He relaxed back in his seat arms folded across his chest and watched them.

"Tell me, Mr. Grantham, what's your background?" Declan waved a hand toward Jess to include her in the question. How the hell had she become involved in security work? He would have thought it was the last type of career she would pursue. Really, he couldn't imagine her settling down to any job—she'd been too wild. But she must be good, otherwise why would his father have employed the company—he only employed the best. He couldn't have known Jess worked for them. No way would his father throw them together again, when he'd gone to such lengths to push them apart.

"I'm ex-army," Grantham said. "We both are."

Army?

No way. His disbelief must have shown because Grantham continued. "Most of the employees at Knight Security have a military background."

He wanted to ask more but it would look weird. He'd get a security check run on her once they'd left. He intended to discover everything about what Jessica Bauer was up to right now. Had she orchestrated this meeting? Maybe she'd had him shot herself, so he'd need a bodyguard… His mind raced ahead of itself, making up more and more far-fetched conspiracy theories.

Jess looked bored now. Staring out of the window, she

tapped her foot on the ground, but a small tic twitched in the side of her cheek. She turned her head slightly and looked him in the face. "Are we done here?"

As she rose to her feet, her jacket swung open, and he caught sight of the shoulder holster and pistol nestled under her arm. Shit, she was for real. Why did the idea of Jess and a gun together make a shiver of apprehension run through him?

Because she hated him. She'd told him so at their last meeting in no uncertain terms. Shouted the words from her hospital bed as he'd turned and walked away from her.

"Mr. McCabe," Grantham said. "I think you should reconsider this. Maybe you aren't feeling quite yourself. You could be in shock from the shooting yesterday."

Oh, he was in shock all right. But not from the shooting. "If I come to my senses, I'll be sure to call."

Jess gave a tight smile. "That will be nice. We'll look forward to it." She turned to Grantham. "Come on, Dave, let's not waste anymore of Mr. McCabe's valuable time. I'm sure he has important bits of paper to play with."

Grantham was back to frowning. He glanced from Declan to Jess and back again, but then gave a shrug. "I think you're making a mistake. But what do I know." He rose to his feet and held out his hand. Declan stood as well and shook it. "Call us if you change your mind."

He sat back down as he watched them walk away. Jess moved with a long stride, her hands shoved in the pockets of her pants, her ponytail swinging. Her hair was longer than it used to be; he was guessing loose it would touch her ass.

An image of that ass naked flashed up in his mind. Smooth and perfect and pointing up at him, thighs parted so he could see the damp blond curls peeking out. His dick twitched. Then the image was overlaid with another memory, and before he could think it was a bad idea, he called out to her, "Jess."

About to open the door, she stopped short—maybe it was the use of her first name—and turned slowly. Her eyes were narrowed. "What?"

He grinned. "Do you still have the tattoo?"

Chapter Three

"Fucking asshole," Jess muttered and slammed the door behind her.

Whirling around, she reached for the door handle, meaning to go back in there and find just what he was playing at.

"Are you going to tell me what that was all about?" Dave asked from beside her.

"No." She forced her hand back to her side. No way was she going back until she had cooled down.

"Come on, Jess. I wouldn't say you have the best of attitudes with clients, but even for you that was over the top."

She opened her mouth to tell him to mind his own bloody business, then snapped it closed again. It was his business, but that didn't mean she was going to tell him anything. What could she tell him anyway? She had no clue what was going on. "He started it."

Dave's lips twitched. "What are we, kindergarten children?"

She shrugged. "Maybe." God, she needed out of there.

Time to get her shit together. She'd brought Dave along in case they needed to start the job immediately. But also as a means of keeping her distance while she'd discovered just what sort of effect meeting Declan again would have.

Catastrophic. That about covered it.

So much for playing nice. But she hadn't expected Declan *not* to recognize her. She hadn't known why he had asked for her, but it had never occurred to her that he hadn't. That he would have no clue it was her. That had thrown her totally off balance.

A whole nasty blast of unwelcome shock had hit her in the solar plexus when he'd said it was his father who had arranged for Knight Security's involvement. Had some little demented part of her brain actually liked the idea that Declan wanted to see her again? Had she imagined some fond memories had driven the action?

Ugh!

Instead, it was Rory McCabe who had contacted them. What the hell was with that? Ten years ago, he'd pretty much ordered her to leave his son alone and never to darken his door again.

Yet he must have known it was her. He'd asked for her by name.

God, her head was going to explode. She tugged at her ponytail trying to ease the pressure.

"I take it you and Mr. Tall-Dark-and-Handsome-Billionaire have history."

Her gaze darted to Dave. "Mind your goddamned business." But she couldn't see that happening. Dave was an atrocious gossip and this would be all around the office within minutes of them getting back.

"And what's with the tattoo?" Dave asked. "You have a tattoo? Where?"

"Nowhere you're ever going to see. Come on, let's get out of here." She nodded to the young man who sat at the desk across the room, trying to look as though he wasn't hanging on their every word. Declan's assistant? At least he didn't have some sexy bimbo secretary. But why should she care?

"Are you sure we shouldn't try again?" Dave said. "I read what little there was in the file and these guys after him mean business. Even if you don't like him, I'm guessing you don't want him dead."

"And maybe you're guessing wrong. Maybe I don't give a toss." Maybe she'd like to shoot him herself. At just what point had he recognized her? She was betting from the moment she walked through the door. And he'd no doubt thought it would be amusing to string her along. He was a better goddamn actor than she was.

"Hmm. And I think you're protesting too much. Very… intriguing."

"Oh bugger off," she muttered and headed for the elevator. She stared straight ahead as they made their way down, but she could almost hear Dave's brain ticking over. No doubt coming up with more and more salubrious scenarios to entertain the entire office.

"Go back to the office and file a report," she said, as the doors slid open. "This job is officially closed."

"Where are you going?" Dave asked, eying her suspiciously.

"For a walk. I need some fresh air." Without waiting for him to answer, she strode across the reception area and out the front door. Once on the street, she hesitated, not knowing where to go.

She should go back to the office and sign in the firearm, but she really did need to clear her head, and in the end she just turned right and started moving, not really paying attention to where she was going.

She purposefully didn't think, just kept walking, while her brain cooled and her thoughts stopped whirling around in her head. When she reached a measure of calm, she slowed her pace and searched around her, settling on a coffee shop across the road.

She ordered an espresso and sat by the window, staring out but not seeing.

Well, that had gone well. As an exercise in moving on, proving that the past had no power over her anymore, it had been a complete disaster. As an exercise in proving she could play nice, it had been even worse.

Declan had changed so much. She could hardly recognize the boy she had known within the self-assured man she had just met. Though he had always been self-assured; it was one of the things that had drawn her to him. Even at eighteen, he'd known exactly who he was and what he wanted. For a little while that had been her. But he hadn't wanted her enough. She hadn't fitted into his plans for his nice tidy future. What had he told her? She was too wild, a disaster waiting to happen. That had been the first time they'd broken up. She'd stolen a car, gone joyriding…

She'd been seventeen at the time. And yeah, she'd been a little out of control. Not bad, just a tiny bit screwed up and filled with a need for excitement away from her tame middle-class upbringing.

When she'd met Declan, he'd seemed the perfect match.

At first sight, he was the ultimate bad boy. Strangely, she'd met his father first. She'd been running with an older crowd, and they'd gotten tickets to a party in one of Rory McCabe's nightclubs. She'd caught his eye, not surprisingly considering her barely there sparkly dress. He'd invited her to his table, plied her with champagne—she had told him she was twenty-one—and even offered her a job dancing in his club. She'd found the attention flattering. Rory McCabe was a handsome man, an older version of Declan.

Then Declan had stormed over to the table and informed his father that she was in fact only seventeen. Declan had known her from school though he was a year ahead of her. Rory had been all for getting the bouncers to throw her out, but when Declan had said he'd take care of it, he'd given his son a knowing look and told him to play safe.

At first, she'd been pissed that he'd spoiled her fun. But soon she'd forgotten all that. Declan was... She sighed as she remembered him that first night. Tall, towering six inches above her five nine, with black hair, overlong so it brushed his shoulders and fell over his forehead, and mesmerizing silver gray eyes.

For all her wildness, she'd hardly ever been kissed, never having found anyone she wanted enough. But with Declan she was lost. He'd walked with her along the embankment, taken his first kiss with her pushed up against the wall, his big body hard against hers, the salt tang of the river in her nostrils. Even now, she couldn't smell the river without being carried back to that night.

She'd have given him everything right then, but he'd bided his time.

And yeah, she'd done some stupid things, but she'd been

young and she wanted to impress him. She'd known he had reservations. At one point, he'd kept away from her for three nights. When he finally came to see her again, he had given in. Taken her to a hotel room and taken her virginity.

She grinned. He'd been totally shocked at that, probably thought she'd been sleeping around.

After that, they hadn't been able to get enough of each other; their coming together had been explosive. For a second, she had a flashback to the feel of his strong, young body, on her, filling her. He'd made love to her over and over again, until she was sore and still wanting more. When he'd left, she'd thought she would do anything just to feel that way again.

There had been a hint of desperation in his lovemaking; she could see that now. Maybe even then he'd planned that she would have no part in his future, the nice, honest, above-board future that his shady father had always intended for him.

She yanked open her bag, pulled out her cell phone, and drummed her fingers on the casing for a moment. If she was back at the office, she would no doubt be able to access a number for Rory McCabe. But she wasn't ready to go back just yet. Instead, she looked up the number of the nightclub where he had spent most of his time.

"Could I speak to Rory McCabe? Tell him it's Jessica Bauer."

She had no clue whether she would be put through. After all, he'd told her never to contact any of them again and Rory McCabe was not known for making empty threats. He'd been a scary figure on the crime scene at one time, but he'd never been caught, and he was now reputedly straight.

But a minute later he came on the line. "Jessica, how lovely to hear from you."

Sarcastic bastard.

"Why?" she asked.

"How are you? It's been a long time."

"Cut the bullshit. Why did you employ Knight Securities to provide protection for Declan? And why did you specifically ask for me?"

"In answer to the first, I wanted the best and your employer has a good reputation."

"And…?"

"And you can imagine my surprise when I did a quick check on the company and you popped up as second in command. I have to admit, I presumed it was a different Jessica Bauer. It was hardly a profession I would have expected for you."

No, he'd probably expected her to be a hooker or a drug-dealer. "Get on with it," she snapped.

"You've changed."

"Really?"

"Okay. My son does not want a bodyguard. He refused to allow me to provide him with one. When I saw your name and realized who you were, I thought he might be intrigued enough to keep you around." He was silent for a few seconds. "And you would be professional enough to keep him alive."

She considered his answer. Did she believe him? It sort of made some logical sense. "You really think they'll try again."

"I know they will. I'll pay you extra if you persuade him to take the protection."

"I don't want your fucking bribes any more now than I did ten years ago." He'd offered her money back then—a lot of money. She still had the check; it was framed and hanging on her bedroom wall to remind her if she ever got nostalgic and felt like falling in love again. "And just how do you expect me to *persuade* him?"

"Whatever you need to do. You could always twist him around your little finger."

"Oh, yeah. Of course I could."

She didn't wait for him to say anything else just shut down the call and sat tapping the phone on the table.

She'd have been okay this morning if the meeting had gone as expected. They could have been polite to one another, he would have said he didn't want the protection and they could have settled the matter in a businesslike manner. Instead, he'd thrown her off-kilter by pretending he didn't recognize her, getting her back up. More than ever, she needed to get him out of her system, needed to take control of her life and her future. Prove to Jake that she could be nice.

So she'd go back, wrap Declan around her little finger—yeah, what alternate universe was Rory McCabe inhabiting—and persuade him to accept Dave and Steve as bodyguards. Then she could leave, knowing she'd acted in a professional manner. And she'd get her promotion and move on with her life.

Sounded like a plan.

She couldn't believe how far she had walked, and she didn't want the time to think—she suspected that she might come up with a few flaws in her plan if she had time to consider it in detail—so she hailed a cab and gave the driver the address of Declan's office building.

It occurred to her that she might have problems getting

back in, that he might have informed the reception desk that she was persona non grata. But when she gave her name, for a second time that day, the woman told her to go right up.

Had he just not bothered to say anything or had he forgotten her as soon as she walked out the door? Or the alternative, that he was expecting her back.

She hated that she had no clue what was going on.

Did he think she had changed?

Personally, she considered she'd changed beyond all recognition. Both internally and externally. There was nothing of that girl left.

The man was still sitting at his desk outside Declan's office like some sort of guard dog. "He's expecting you. Go right in."

"He is?"

Was she so fucking predictable?

A smile quirked his lips as though he could read her mind. "Reception called up."

"Oh."

God, she was overreacting. She stood in front of the oak door and took some deep breaths, closed her eyes, and forced herself to calmness, something she'd learned to do when on active duty and she needed to focus her thoughts.

Then she pushed open the door and stepped inside. Declan stood by the window, his back to her. The first time around, she hadn't taken in her surroundings. Now she studied the office, maybe to give herself a bit more time. It was spacious, with a huge desk, where Declan had sat at the previous meeting, across one corner. Decorated in cream and black with a long black leather sofa against the wall. Overall the office gave the impression of serenity and good taste. A total opposite to his father's clubs, but hadn't that been what they were aiming for? Respectability.

She took a few more paces into the room, her footsteps muffled on the thick cream carpet. Declan had taken off his jacket; it was slung over the back of his chair and his shirt-sleeves were rolled up. Through the thin silk of his shirt, she could make out the bandage wrapped around his upper arm.

He'd been shot.

Her breath hitched and a sharp pain jabbed at her chest. Someone had actually tried to kill him.

Before, it had seemed unreal. Now, it sank in, and she realized that no, she really didn't want anyone to kill him, however much she hated him.

At eighteen, he'd still had a boyish lankiness to his frame. That was gone. His shoulders had broadened, though his hips were still lean and his legs beneath the charcoal-gray pants were long. His black hair was cut short, and while she watched, he ran a hand through it. He'd always done that when he was thinking, and it would leave him all sexily tousled. Now, it was too short to tousle.

Even from behind, he seemed controlled, contained, all that energy she had loved so much leashed in tight.

Maybe she'd had a lucky escape.

Declan's path in life had been decided early on. His family had always expected him to take the business and make it respectable; that's what he'd been groomed for and he'd gone along with the plan without a hitch. Except for her. And that had been a minor mistake, easily remedied.

After what seemed like an age, he turned around. His hands shoved into his pockets, he scrutinized her from head to toe. A tremor ran through her, but she stiffened her spine and returned the favor. And her breath caught again. It wasn't fair; he was still the most beautiful man she had ever seen.

"You came back," Declan murmured.

"Your father offered me a lot of money."

He raised a brow. "You spoke to him?"

"Well, he would hardly be able to offer me money if I hadn't."

His lips twitched. "I'd forgotten that sarcastic mouth of yours."

"Not the only thing you've forgotten, I'm guessing."

His gaze drifted down over her body, sending shivers across her skin. "You'd be surprised."

What the hell did that mean? "Actually, I turned him down."

"You did? And yet here you are."

Time to get nice. She took a deep breath, curved her lips into a smile. "I like to think we were friends once." *Until you dumped me.* "You're in danger and I want to help. Why not reconsider? Take the bodyguards—they'll be discreet. They won't cramp your style."

"And would you be one of those bodyguards?"

Not a chance in hell. "If you want me to be."

His eyes narrowed, and he studied her face for a long minute. "Are you trying to be nice?"

She gritted her teeth. "Yes."

He let out a short laugh. "I'd forgotten your habit of absolute honesty. But you suck at the nice thing."

"No, I don't." She shrugged. "I'm just a little out of practice."

He took a step closer, his gaze still wandering over her.

"You're staring," she said. And she wished he would stop.

She was used to being stared at, and she'd learned to ignore it. But somehow she couldn't ignore Declan's cool scrutiny.

He took another step closer, so close she could breathe in his scent—warm man, and some expensive cologne, sharp and citrusy. She stared straight ahead, but that meant she was gazing at his chest and she could see the dark shadow of his nipples beneath the thin silk. Her mouth went dry, and she forced her eyes upward just as he reached out and ran a finger down the scar on her face. A shiver rippled through her at his light touch, settling low down in her belly.

"Did you get this in the army?" he asked.

She frowned, too shocked by the effect of his touch to make sense of the words at first. He must be quite aware of where she'd got the scar. He'd visited her in the hospital after the crash. That was when he'd told her they were finished. "I got it in the accident before you left."

His hand dropped to his side, and he took a step back, his gaze fixed on her cheek, so for the first time in years she had the urge to raise her hand and cover the scar. Instead, she clenched her fists at her side.

"They told me you weren't seriously hurt," he muttered.

"I wasn't. This is nothing."

He shook his head. "I remember now. You had a bandage on your face, but they told me you were okay. They said just cuts and bruises. You should have told me."

"It is just a cut—from the broken windshield." Why was he making such a big deal about it?

"You didn't have it taken care of?"

"You mean plastic surgery?" When he nodded, she continued, "Didn't seem worth it. At first…" Shit, what was she supposed to say—that she'd been too broken inside to worry about what the outside looked like? Then later, once she was in the army, she just hadn't thought about it. Now, she actually liked the scar. Kim had told her it gave her character. Without it, she'd just be one more beautiful woman, and what was the point in that?

But from the shock on Declan's face, maybe that was all she had been to him. She gave a mirthless smile. "Your father told me all I'd had going was my looks and I'd fucked that up."

"He did. When?"

Maybe his father hadn't told him about their last meeting; maybe he hadn't thought it important enough to mention.

"I went to see you after I got out of hospital. Of course you had already fled the country." She gave what she hoped was a dismissive shrug.

"He didn't tell me."

She'd always suspected as much. "What would have been the point? You'd made your feelings—or lack of them—perfectly clear."

He turned away and strolled across the room. "You want a drink? I need a drink." He glanced back over his shoulder. "Not often you get shot one day and faced with a specter from the past the next."

"A specter?"

He stopped in front of a cabinet, opened it, and examined the contents. After pulling out two shot glasses, he poured a measure of scotch into both, then headed to the sofa, placing the glasses down on the coffee table. He picked up one and tossed the amber liquid down in one go. He strode back and picked up the bottle, brought it with him this time and topped off his glass. "Well?"

"Should you be drinking and taking medication? Not very sensible."

He studied her, head cocked to one side. "Since when did you get sensible?"

"When I joined the army. It was a painful process."

"I'll bet." Something flickered in his silver eyes. "I'm still trying to come to terms with the idea of you in uniform. I'm not sure whether it terrifies me or turns me on. Actually, I take that back…"

"It terrifies you?"

"You wish." He waved a hand at the sofa. "Sit down, and you can try and persuade me into those bodyguards while you have your drink."

What the hell? She'd already decided she wasn't going back to the office that afternoon. She'd put in so much over-time in the last couple of months, she deserved an afternoon off. And she still needed to do what she had come here for. Prove he was out of her system and move on. Oh, and be nice.

She'd never been one for self-delusion, but as she edged around him and perched in the corner of the sofa, she had the strangest feeling that she was doing just that. Reaching out, she wrapped her hand around the glass then brought it to her lips. They'd drunk a lot of scotch together; it had been her drink of choice at seventeen. Declan's kisses had often tasted of scotch, expensive malt he'd filched from his dad's personal supply.

She hadn't touched scotch since, and now as the warm liquid flooded her mouth it brought back memories of those kisses. Sweet and hot and…better forgotten.

He was still standing. Jess frowned up at him, and he came around and sank down onto the sofa beside her. So close, she could feel the heat of his big body.

The scotch was warming her inside now. Maybe this hadn't been a good idea, but she couldn't bring herself to get up and move.

Declan settled back in the seat and stretched his long legs out in front of him. He sipped his second drink in what should have been companionable silence, but in fact the air thrummed with tension and she was totally aware of his body so close to hers.

She tried to tell herself that this was normal. "This" being the hot, heavy heat between her thighs. She had a past with this man. She'd had the most amazing multiple orgasms with him. It was obvious that being this close to him was going to make her think about sex. She was a normal woman—though a lot of people might laugh at that—and this was a normal woman's reaction.

Well, a normal, frustrated woman's reaction.

How long was it since she'd had a man? In the early years she'd tried a few times, picked up some stranger, gone home with him. The sex had been okay, but had never lived up to what she'd had before, and the whole experience had felt tainted, not right, and she'd given up in the end. There had been no one since she left the army. That was over five years. And in that time she'd made do with her vibrator and believed she'd never missed sex. Yeah, definitely deluded.

She cast him a swift sideways peek. He was watching her out of heavy-lidded eyes. He caught her glance and slowly raised his glass.

"To old times."

Then he gently placed the glass on the table and reached for her.

Chapter Four

No way.

Jess slammed her glass down on the table beside his, the scotch sloshing over her fingers. She jumped to her feet as his hand touched her arm and then put the sofa between them. Declan turned to look at her and something glinted in his eyes. Amusement maybe.

She gritted her teeth. Did the bastard find her funny?

Much as she really wanted to make some cutting remark, she decided that just this once, she was going to keep her mouth firmly closed and make a dignified retreat. A fast, dignified retreat. She backed away a few steps as he pushed himself to his feet.

"Going somewhere?" he murmured.

She licked her lips. His eyes followed the movement and something hot and dark settled in her stomach. She cleared her throat. "Well, this has been nice. Old times and all that, but I must get back to the office."

"But you haven't convinced me I need protecting, yet."

"You haven't convinced me you're worth protecting," she snapped.

His lips twitched at the corners, and she got the distinct impression he liked her loss of control. "Good to see the old Jess is still there."

Why the hell would he think that was good? He'd run a mile—thousands of miles actually—from the old Jess. "No, she's not." She whirled around and stalked for the door.

She could sense him watching her. Expected him to try to stop her. But of course he didn't.

As his office door closed behind her for a second time, she heaved a sigh of… Actually, she wasn't sure what it was a sigh of. Hopefully relief, but she suspected disappointment. What had she wanted to happen in there? She was supposed to be proving to herself that she didn't care, that she was ready to move on, that he meant nothing to her. Instead, her skin felt sensitive, her nipples were tight, and she was uncomfortably aware of the moist heat soaking her panties. And he hadn't even touched her.

She'd forgotten what desire felt like. A craving in the blood. A deep need to sink into sensation and never come up for air.

Someone cleared their throat. Declan's assistant was studying her from behind his desk. He looked amused as well. Christ, she was a laugh a minute today.

"What?" she asked.

"Nothing. Do you need another appointment?"

"No. I won't be coming back." She said it more for her benefit than his. She'd just have to find another way to persuade Jake she could do his job. Keeping her pace slow and controlled, she crossed to the elevator. She didn't want to look rattled. All the same, she couldn't stop the nervous tap of her boot against the carpet as she waited, totally aware of the doors behind her. She didn't turn as she heard them open.

"Come on," she muttered to the elevator. She huffed out a breath of relief as the doors finally slid open. Stepping inside, she stabbed her finger on the down button. The doors were closing as Declan stopped them with a hand. He stepped in beside her, filling the small space, and the doors closed, sealing them in together.

Her stomach lurched as they started to descend. She took a deep breath. No time to be a wimp. "Was there something else you wanted?"

"Oh yeah." The low, husky tone sent shivers through her. Her gaze flashed to his face, but his expression was blank.

She crossed her arms over her chest and attempted a bored expression. "And that would be?"

"I want to know why you came here today. I had no clue, but you were expecting me. So why did you come?"

"Why not? You were just another job."

"Don't lie. And why come back a second time…Why do you care if I take the protection or not?"

Maybe it was time to inject a little truth. "I'm in line for a promotion. My boss said if I impress you, I get the job."

"Impress me?"

"Yeah, you know…be nice." She shrugged. "He reckons I have an attitude problem."

"Really?" His lips quirked. They were facing each other now. His gaze ran over her, and she had to hold herself still to prevent a little squirm, and then his eyes narrowed as he locked gazes with her.

She shrugged again. "But don't worry. If you're determined not to accept the bodyguards, there's nothing I can do about it."

"I wouldn't be so sure." He took a step toward her, filling her personal space. "You don't want to…try a little harder to persuade me?"

The door opened and two men made to enter. Declan turned his head. "Don't even think about it," he said quietly, and the men backed away and the doors closed once more. "Where were we?"

"I was on my way out?"

He tossed her a glance and then pressed the elevator button. They started to rise.

"What the fuck?" she muttered.

"Just a little experiment. Come on, Jess, where's your sense of adventure?"

His hand reached out, then slipped around the back of her neck. He tilted her head so she had no choice but to look into his face. Actually, she did have a choice; she had a gun, and she could shoot him. Instead, she held herself very still as he lowered his face to hers. Maybe this was what she needed to prove once and for all that she was over him. Or maybe she was a self-deluding idiot with no sense of self-preservation who just wanted a snog.

His lips were warm and firm and his tongue tasted of scotch, the flavor intoxicating, as he pushed inside, filling her. His kiss deepened, hot and wet and hard. One hand was still at her nape, the other wrapped around her, cupping her ass, pulling her against his hard length so she was aware of him against her breasts, her belly, her hips. Heat shot through her, thrills shivering along her nerves, pooling in her sex, taking her back to those long ago days, when she'd loved him and he'd taken everything she had to give and then dumped her when daddy told him to.

How dare he? How the hell fucking dare he kiss her? And not just kiss her, but kiss her like he fucking cared. Like she was the only woman in the goddamn world. He had always made her feel like that. No other man had come close.

And she hated it. She could feel herself spiraling out of control, the old feelings building inside her. All mixed in with an almost overwhelming need, to have him inside her just one more time. Have that hard body on her, in her.

They were almost glued together, and she shoved her hands between them, pushing hard. When he still didn't budge, she bit down on his lower lip, then placed her fingers around his upper arm and squeezed the exact spot he'd taken a bullet.

"Ouch." Raising his head, he loosened his grip and stepped back. His eyes were narrowed and a tic jumped in his cheek. He wasn't as cool as he was pretending. "You always did like it rough," he murmured.

"Fuck off, Declan."

His gaze dropped to her body. She acted instinctively and peered down; her nipples were tight little peaks. He smirked. "You're definitely getting…nicer. I might even be persuaded to put a good word in with your boss."

"Thanks, but don't put yourself out." Jess gritted her teeth. Had he always been this annoying? "Actually, there is another reason I came back."

"There is?"

"Hmm." She copied his actions and allowed her gaze to drop down over his body, God he was gorgeous. Why did

he have to be the most gorgeous man she had ever encountered? "You know I hate you, Declan. I've hated you for a
long time. Too long."

He swiped his tongue across his lower lip. "Baby girl, I
love the way you hate."

"Don't call me that." She'd always hated the way he
called her baby girl. She was only a year younger than him.
"And hating you is pointless, and I've wasted too much time
on it. So yeah, I came today, thought I'd take a look, remind
myself of what an arrogant prick you are, and then I'd wipe
you from my mind and move on." She stepped up closer and
prodded him in the chest. He was like iron. "And guess what,
Declan? You're an arrogant prick."

"So you want to move on?"

"Yeah. I'm going to find me a nice man."

He laughed. He actually laughed at her, and her palm
itched with the need to reach for her gun. "Baby girl, you
wouldn't know what to do with a nice man. And he sure as
hell wouldn't know what to do with you."

"And you do, I suppose?" She knew the words were a
mistake as soon as they escaped from her mouth.

"Oh yeah."

Heat coiled in her belly, and she swallowed, her mouth
suddenly dry. They were no longer moving. The lift had come
to a halt at Declan's floor. But the doors remained closed.

"Come back with me, Jess." He leaned in close and
kissed the side of her neck and heat in her belly sank lower.
He licked her pulse point with the tip of his tongue and she
swayed. "Come on, Jess." The words whispered across her
skin. "You know you want to. One last time, just to remind
you of how awful it was…boring and messy and then we can

both move on."

The desire was building. Maybe this is what she needed. One last time. She'd never trust him again, never allow herself to care for him, risk any of her feelings. But this wasn't about feelings; this was about shagging. At the thought, her sex clenched tight.

God, she wanted him.

All of him. Then she wanted to walk away and never look back.

He must have seen something in her face because a slow smile curled his lips and his eyes glittered.

He pressed the button to open the door and then grabbed her hand, his fingers twining with hers as though he were still not sure she wouldn't make a dash for it.

Neither was she.

She was working on autopilot; she'd shut down the parts of her brain that could actually think. Because deep down she was perfectly aware that this was a mistake of fucking awesome proportions.

He dragged her out of the elevator and across the office. His assistant was still behind the desk, but his mouth had fallen open.

"Go home," Declan said. "You're finished for the day."

He didn't wait for any response, just continued to tug her across the carpeted floor and then through the big double doors into his office. The doors clicked shut behind them, and Declan turned and flicked the lock, then moved to face her.

"Take off the gun."

She shook her head. "What?"

"The gun, Jess. Take it off. You hate me, remember? I

don't want you tempted if I piss you off."

Her brows drew together. "And are you planning on pissing me off?"

He grinned. "Well, it's not on my immediate list, but from past experience I can't rule it out."

Yeah, they'd always been volatile, had spent as much time arguing as they had making love.

They were going to do this. She knew that. There was no turning back now—if *he* tried, she might very well hold him down and take him by force. Years of need were simmering beneath the surface. She *had* to have this.

Keeping her eyes on him, she stripped off her jacket, strolled across the office, and laid it on a nearby chair. Then she slowly undid the buckles on the holster, slipped it from her shoulder, and gently rested it on top of the jacket.

He was watching her, his gaze intent, fixed on her like a predator searching for weaknesses in its prey. He appeared outwardly calm, but she could sense the pent-up emotion beneath the surface waiting to explode. A strange primordial fear gripped her, and she held herself still as though she might set off some cataclysmic explosion with the wrong move.

She tried to remind herself that he was a boring businessman who spent his whole life sitting behind a desk, but the description wouldn't hold. He'd always had an almost savage masculine beauty, his face all harsh angles, sharp cheekbones, the hard line of his jaw, the fierce slash of his black brows.

Her gaze dropped, snagging on the bulge at his groin. He wanted her.

And she wanted him with a desperation that scared her

witless. The last working cell in her brain screamed at her to run. But she wasn't a coward. At the thought, that one functioning brain cell snorted in disgust. She was looking for any excuse to stay.

But it was just sex. Sex didn't have to mean anything. She'd proved that. Just not with this man. Yet. But wasn't that why she'd come here, to prove he was no different?

She was overthinking. She didn't want to think. She wanted to feel.

Their abandoned drinks were still on the table and she strode over, picked up her glass, and swallowed it in one go. She felt the scotch in her belly, stoking the flames. She slammed the glass down and picked up Declan's, gulped that, and turned to face him.

He quirked a brow but didn't speak. Instead, he raised his hand and slowly unbuttoned his shirt, tugging it out of his pants, stripping it off, and dropping it to the floor. And she stood there like an idiot and stared. A white bandage crossed his shoulder breaking up the perfection of his olive skin. His chest was smooth, but beneath his navel, a line of dark hair disappeared into his pants.

As she watched, he unbuckled the leather belt and flicked open the button on his pants.

Holy shit.

Sweat broke out on her palms, and she resisted the urge to wipe them down her sides. The alcohol was a buzz in her brain quieting the niggles of doubt. She placed the glass she was still gripping gently on the desk. If this was going to happen, she wanted it on her terms. She would decide.

Her gaze snagged on the line of silky black hair running down his lean belly, disappearing… Yeah, it was going to happen.

As she accepted that fact, a smile tugged at her mouth.

Holy hell. She was going to have sex. With Declan. She was going to fuck his brains out and then this time, she would be the one to walk away.

She stalked toward him, her gaze fixed on the bulge in his pants. It was huge, and it was all hers. For as long as she wanted. Which wouldn't be very long. Because, while she might be deluded, she wasn't a total idiot.

· · ·

Somewhere in the last thirty seconds, she had reached a decision. Before that, he'd been in no way sure of her.

Now she was coming for him.

Fear twisted inside him. The sensation tightened his balls, sent blood pooling to his groin. She'd always been so passionate. Crazy passionate. The intensity of her feelings had woken needs inside him he'd spent his life controlling. Even at seventeen, she'd often been the one to initiate their lovemaking, teasing him, testing him, trying to push him over the edge.

She came to a halt in front of him. God she was beautiful. One hand reached out, laid flat against his heart. Could she feel its frantic beat? Of course, she could. He held himself very still as she scraped her nails down his chest, then tucked one finger in his waistband.

"You sure you want to do this?" she murmured. "Aren't you afraid Daddy will find out?"

No, he wasn't. For some reason his father had orchestrated this meeting. He would find out why—but later. "I think Daddy gave you to me as a present."

A frown flickered across her face; he was guessing the thought had occurred to her as well, but she banished it with a little shake of her head. She moved the hand that hovered over his groin and flicked a finger at the bandage on his shoulder. "And he had you gift wrapped for me. Nice."

He'd had enough talk. He ached to be inside her. His dick was so hard, it pressed painfully against his fly, and holding her gaze he lowered his zipper, groaned at the relief.

Her tongue flashed out across her plump lower lip, leaving it glistening with moisture and his cock jerked in the confines of his boxers. He groaned again and her eyes flicked down, and then she closed the last distance between them.

Without touching him anywhere else, she went up on tiptoes and licked along his lower lip as she had done her own. Then she pressed her mouth against his and her body pushed up against him. Her arms locked on his shoulders, and she dragged him down and kissed him. The kiss was fierce—he could sense the barely leashed anger—and she shoved her tongue into his mouth as though she was fucking him. She'd always wanted to be the one in control, but he had always wrested it from her. Now he cupped her jaw in his hand, angled her chin, and took charge of the kiss. His tongue fought with hers, filling her mouth, taking possession.

She gave way beneath the pressure of his kiss, and he backed her up until she was against the wall, then kissed her some more, hot, wet kisses as though he could devour her, ravage her with his mouth and she gave as good as she got. Biting at his lips, fingernails digging into his shoulder.

He needed more, needed all of her. His free hand shifted between them, tearing at the buttons on her shirt so they scattered. At last, he pulled back from the kiss, his breathing ragged. He stared down at her; her skin was pale, almost luminescent, her breasts swelling above the plain white bra, her nipples pressing at the cotton. He lowered his head, nipped one with his teeth, and her back arched. She'd always liked her sex tinged with a little pain. Had said it made her feel alive. He bit down, harder this time, felt her hips jerk against him.

He tugged the shirt down her shoulders and dropped it to the floor, then slipped a hand behind her back and flicked open the catch on her bra, tossing it after the shirt. Her breasts were small but perfect, her nipples pink and swollen. He licked one until it glistened, then sucked the other into his mouth, and her spine arched again.

He rubbed his cock against her belly until his balls were close to exploding. He needed to be inside her and soon. First, there was something he wanted to see. He opened the button at her waist, lowered the zipper, and stroked the soft skin of her flat belly. As his fingers encountered the softness of her curls, he stopped.

"Turn around," he murmured.

"What?" She sounded dazed, her eyelids fluttering.

"I want to see if you still belong to me."

"I never belonged to you." But the words lacked force and she allowed him to turn her slowly. He sank to his knees behind her, then tugged her pants down around her hips, taking the white cotton panties with them.

His cock pulsed—she had a lovely ass, round but firm and decorated with his name. Declan was written in fancy script and surrounded by black roses across her left buttock. He trailed a finger over it as his mind flew back to the night she'd gotten the tattoo done. How he'd tried not to be turned on by the fact she was getting his name inked onto her ass. She'd wanted him to get one as well, but he'd refused. Afterward, he'd taken her back to a hotel room and fucked her from behind because she was too sore to lie on her back.

He'd liked it that she'd marked herself as his, even while he'd known the ink would last far longer than the relationship.

Then he looked closer and went still. Something had been added to the tattoo, words almost hidden in the swirls surrounding it. He sat back on his heels. "Declan is a prick? You had *Declan is a prick* tattooed on your ass?"

He glanced up. She was peering at him over her shoulder, a smirk on her face. "I thought about getting it removed, but this seemed easier and somehow appropriate."

"Witch." Leaning closer, he kissed his name, then bit down hard on her soft flesh, felt a shiver run through her. He massaged the globes of her ass, then ran his hands down the long slender length of her thighs. She shifted, her stance widening and he breathed in the hot scent of excited woman. Even if she thought him a prick, she still wanted him. She raised her ass a little, as if offering it to him and he stroked back up, slipping his fingers inside until they met the warm heat of her sex. She was drenched, and he ran one finger over the length of her, finding her clit swollen with need. He circled the little nub, not quite touching, and her hips bucked against him. He pushed one finger inside. She was tight but so slick he entered easily, groaning as her muscles clamped around him. He rubbed at her inner walls, found the spot that had always driven her wild, and pressed upward. A gasp escaped her, and she moaned as he withdrew.

He straightened, then turned her to face him. A flush marked the pale skin of her cheeks, and her dark eyes glittered. Her pants were caught around her legs and she kicked them off, taking her boots with them to leave her naked. Every muscle in his body clenched tight.

His gaze ran down her body, the thrust of her breasts, slender waist, the white-blond curls, the lean flat belly. She was toned, almost muscular. He loved it. He was used to soft women and there was nothing soft about Jess. He reached for her, but she held up a hand to stop him.

Shit, she wasn't going to back out now was she? He'd let her go but it would kill him.

"Condom," she muttered.

He couldn't believe he'd almost forgotten. Well, at least he could be sure she wasn't trying to trap him into anything. He left her for a moment, went to his chair where he'd discarded his jacket, and pulled a foil packet from the inner pocket.

She watched him as he pushed his pants down over his hips, drawing in a breath as he pulled his dick free. Her eyes never left him as he rolled the condom down over his length.

His hands gripped her hips and he lifted her. "Put your legs around my waist."

She complied, and he felt the wet heat of her sex against his cock. He gripped her ass with both hands and backed her up a little, so her shoulders rested against the wall, and then he shifted her slightly. His cock slid against her wetness, and she rubbed against him trying to get closer.

He held her still with his hands at her hips. "Say you want me."

Her eyes flashed open, and she glared at him.

"Say you want me and you can have me. Just three little words."

He didn't know why he was pushing it, but he needed to hear her say the words despite the fact that it was obvious she wanted him. He'd always made her say it—it had been a ritual between them. Maybe his proof that he was the one in control.

When she remained silent, her teeth clamped on her lower lip, he shifted her slightly, rubbing his cock against her clit. And her mouth parted on a moan.

"I want you...prick."

It was enough. His hands tightened on her buttocks, he lifted her, his cock homed in on where it needed to be, and he shoved into her in one hard lunge. It had been ten years, but his body remembered the feel of her wrapped so tight around him.

He knew how she liked it: hard and fast, and he held her in place against the wall as he pulled almost all the way out and then slammed into her. He needed her to come and fast because he wasn't going to last long and on the next stroke, he ground against her clit. He pulled her harder against him, repeated the move over and over until he could feel the tension inside her.

Lowering his head, he sucked a nipple into his mouth as he slid out of her, biting down on the inward stroke, suckling as he used his grip on her ass to rotate against her clit and she came apart in his arms. Her head fell back, and she screamed.

He loosened his control and pumped into her as she spasmed around him, loving the contractions pulling at his cock. The pressure was building in his balls, his spine. He opened his eyes and stared into her beautiful face as pleasure swelled inside him, bursting, flooding him and he burrowed his face in the side of her neck. Finally, when the tremors stopped, he raised his head and stared down at her. Her eyes were closed.

"I still hate you," she said.

Chapter Five

Holy shit. Crap. Bugger.

Her legs were around his waist, his hands hot on her arse, which was just as well because she was pretty sure he was all that was holding her up. And if he let her go, she would melt into a puddle at his feet.

And that was so not going to happen.

She'd spoken the truth. She hated him. Hated that he seemed to be the only man capable of making her feel this way.

Weak.

She gritted her teeth and opened her eyes. The light was bright, probably because outside it was broad daylight and she was in an office with floor-to-ceiling windows and no blinds. She gazed out at the sky as an alternative to looking closer to home.

Yes, she hated him, and already her body craved him again. After he'd left her the last time, she'd gone through withdrawal symptoms similar to a drug addict. Had lost herself for a while. She would not go through that again.

As Declan's hands tightened on her ass, a ripple of re-sidual pleasure ran through her and she winced. He was still lodged firmly inside her, filling her, stretching her. The old Declan had had amazing stamina. She had no intention of sticking around to find out whether or not that had changed.

"Put me down."

His fingers dug into the flesh of her buttocks and for a moment, she thought she was going to have to resort to physical assault. She was pretty sure she could take Declan if she had the element of surprise. He was bigger, stronger, but she was betting she was faster and she had a black belt in Tae Kwon Do. And his pants around his ankles were hardly likely to help his case. She was filled with a need to strike out, to release some of her pent-up feelings.

She tensed her muscles, a quick punch to the chest, twist free…

Before she could act on the impulse, he lifted her up slightly, pulling out. A sense of loss washed over her. Ignoring it, she loosened her legs from around his waist and put her feet on the ground. She'd avoided looking at his face; now she risked a glance. A sleepy, sated expression filled his eyes, but otherwise, his face was blank. She couldn't blame him. So was hers. She hoped. Steadying her legs, she let go of his shoulders. She could stand alone. Declan took a step back, reached down, and pulled up his pants, fastening the zipper but not bothering with anything else. He shoved his hands in his pockets and scrutinized her. His gaze dropped to her body, her totally bare-assed naked body, and his nostrils flared.

"You're beautiful."

The murmured words twisted things low down in her body. She ignored the sensation, because getting all happy because Declan thought her beautiful was a big mistake. Not quite as huge as fucking him against his office wall, but big. "Glad you think so."

"You shouldn't have come back if you didn't want this to happen."

She scowled. "Who said I didn't want it to happen? There's nothing like a nice screw against the wall to cement client relations."

A small smile curled his sensual lips. "Don't lie. It's been a long time for you."

And how the fuck did he know that?

"You were desperate," he murmured as though she'd asked the question out loud. "And so tight it was almost like the first time."

"I don't remember."

"Liar."

"Yeah, well, you were pretty damn desperate yourself."

He shrugged. "I was curious. You were the best fuck I'd ever had even at seventeen. What you lacked in experience, you made up for in enthusiasm."

She glared daggers at him, imagined him lying at her feet. It could be arranged. "Well, glad I indulged your curiosity."

"Glad to see you're still as enthusiastic."

Shit, she hated him. Had she mention that little fact? Was it worth saying again?

But she didn't like the way he was looking at her. His gaze focused on her breasts now, then lower and she had to fight the urge to cover herself. She'd never been body conscious, but this was self-protection.

She'd promised herself she could have him once. Now it was time to get out of there. Purge Declan and the old negative emotions from her brain, take control of her life, and move on.

She bent down, scooped up her clothes from the floor, slipped out from in front of him, and strolled across the office.

"I can't believe you had 'Declan is a prick' tattooed on your ass."

At the words, she glanced back over her shoulder. "If the name fits." It had been on a drunken night out with some of her army buddies. They'd all gone for tattoos, but Jess hadn't wanted a new one. In fact, she didn't want the old one, so she'd just changed it a little.

Ignoring the looming man, she pulled on her underwear, her pants, and shirt—most of the buttons were gone, but she tucked it in as well as she could—then sat down to put on her boots. Finally, she picked up her holster and slipped it over her shoulder, fastened the buckles, and felt ready to face him. He hadn't moved. Still stood there with his hands in his pockets, watching her. She returned the inspection. He must work out—he was ripped—no way would he get a body like that from sitting at a desk all day. Weights she reckoned. He'd certainly picked her up with ease.

But it would take more than a nice body to impress her. A nice body and a stunning face and a huge…

She shook her head and picked up her jacket. Definitely time to get out of there. Pulling her jacket on to cover the gun, she turned back to him. "So, as you don't need a bodyguard…" Her gaze drifted to the bandage on his arm, proof that he obviously did need a bodyguard. A little twinge of something stabbed her in the gut. Fear? Guilt? But if he didn't want babysitting, there was nothing she could do about it. She couldn't force him. "I'll cancel your account and"—she gave a casual shrug—"that's it.

Lovely seeing you again after all these years. Try not to get shot and maybe we'll do it again in another ten." *Or maybe not.*

He didn't speak as she strolled across the room. The skin down her spine prickled as she waited for him to say something, anything. She didn't know what she wanted him to say, but the silence was deafening.

Until she reached the door. As she opened it to leave, he spoke.

"You can tell your boss that I think you were very…nice."

Ha, so he thought she was nice. Slimy bastard. What right did he have to think she was nice after dumping her unceremoniously all those years ago? Even after a night of trying to put them from her mind, the words still niggled as she entered the office the following morning.

She sort of forgot them as she walked through the big open-plan room that housed the operatives who weren't out on assignment or who were about to head out. Everyone's eyes followed her movements. Her gaze snagged on Dave, seated at a desk, arms folded, a smug grin on his face. Her eyes narrowed. If he wasn't careful, he'd be spending the next six months on the most boring surveillance jobs she could come up with.

Her, vindictive? Hell, yes.

She stalked across the room, stabbed her finger on the elevator button, and tapped her feet on the tiled floor. As the elevator doors opened, someone spoke from behind. "Are you going to show us this tattoo, Jess?"

She turned slowly, headed back the way she had come, halted in front of Steve, who had a cocky grin on his face.

"Do you really want to piss off your soon-to-be-boss?" she asked sweetly.

The grin faded, but his eyes still gleamed with amusement. "No, boss."

"Well, don't mention tattoos again."

"Yes, boss."

She resigned herself to more hazing as she made her way up to Jake's office; she'd known Dave wouldn't keep quiet about the comment. There was no one in the outer office and she banged on the door and waited for the muffled come-in. It wasn't safe to enter Jake's office these days without knocking first.

But when she opened the door, Jake wasn't there. Instead Kim, his wife, sat behind his desk, long legs stretched out, her feet resting on the dark mahogany.

She looked positively radiant; marriage to Jake obviously agreed with her. Jess had known Kim for nearly five years now, since Jake had rescued her from her bastard of a husband and given her a job at Knight Securities. She'd always found it hard to relate to women, but Kim and her other best friend Dani were special. Though at this moment she didn't appear particularly friendly; her mouth was a tight line and she studied Jess through narrowed eyes.

"You have a tattoo, and you didn't tell me?"

She shrugged. "It never came up in conversation."

"How come I've never seen it?"

"Probably because we've never gotten naked together."

"True." She pursed her lips. "Has Dani seen it?"

"Yes?"

"So you've gotten naked with Dani but not with me?"

"Obviously." Actually, Dani had been one of the army

buddies who'd all gotten tattoos together the night she'd had hers…updated. "Where's Jake?"

"Delayed. He said to start without him." This was their weekly meeting to go through all the open cases and make sure the staff was allocated where best suited. "And don't try and change the subject. You know you're not getting out of here until I've seen it."

She sighed. "Okay. But you're not to tell anyone." She wouldn't give the assholes the satisfaction. Let them guess. "And I mean not *anyone*."

"Not even Jake?"

"Especially not Jake."

Kim's eyes widened as Jess unfastened her pants, slipped them down, then turned her back, and pulled up the edge of her panties to reveal her left buttock.

"Declan?" Kim said. "I can't believe you had some guy's name tattooed on your bottom. You hate men."

"He was my first boyfriend. I got it done when I was seventeen. Look a bit closer."

Kim got to her feet and came around the desk. She leaned in and let out a giggle. "Is a prick."

"I got that bit added a little while later." She pulled up her pants. "Now that's all cleared up, can I get to work?"

"Hmm. Jake left you a note."

She took the piece of paper Kim held out and unfolded it.

I hear the job was canceled—what happened to "playing nice?"

And you have a tattoo?

"Fuck," she muttered.

Kim gave her a sympathetic smile. "He talked to Dave when he got back yesterday."

Oh well, she'd known it was bound to happen. But no way was Gary getting her promotion. She'd find another way to prove she was nice. If it killed her. She peered up at her best friend as she leaned against the desk. "Am I nice?"

Kim snorted. Then coughed and cleared her throat. "Of course you're nice. Would I be best friends with someone who wasn't…nice?"

"You're lying." Christ, even her best friend didn't think she was nice. Was she aiming too high? She flung herself into the chair. Actually, there was something she needed Kim's help with, might as well make use of her while she was here. "Have you got a few minutes?"

"As long as you need."

She took a deep breath. "I joined a dating agency."

"When? Where? How? I don't believe you."

"It's really your fault—well, yours, and Dani's. I figured if the two of you could find someone, then so could I. But it's a load of crap. The guys I've met so far are…boring."

"And you want…exciting?"

"No, I've done exciting and I've no plans to repeat the experience."

"Declan, I presume."

"Yeah. Anyway what I want is nice." Oh God, that word again. It was taking over her life. "But I need to be able to spend time with them and stay awake. Anyway, I'll give it one more try, but I thought I'd adjust my criteria."

"And strike boring off the list."

"Something like that."

Kim shook her head. "I can't believe you didn't tell me. First the tattoo, now this." She peered at her closely. "What other secrets are you hiding?"

"None. And I'm telling you now. I thought you could have a quick look at my questionnaire on the dating site, see where I'm going wrong."

Kim rubbed her hands together. "No problem. Get me in there."

Jess sat in Jake's chair and pulled up the dating agency forms on the screen in front of her, then stood up so Kim could take the seat.

"So what I thought—"

Kim cut her off with a wave of her hand. "Just leave it to me. I've got this."

Jess paced the room, hands shoved in her pockets as Kim's fingers flew across the keyboard. What the hell was she writing? Maybe this was a huge mistake. After all, Kim was hardly an expert on the subject of dating. One abusive husband and then Jake—hardly a wealth of experience.

She peered over her shoulder, but Kim waved her away again. "You are such a total fibber," she said.

"Am not." Well maybe just a little. But who'd want her if she told the truth?

"I can't believe you've put cooking down as an interest," Kim muttered.

Jess scowled. "I can make really good coffee. And I thought I'd attract a better class of man if I came across as domesticated."

Kim snorted. "There, done. No don't look. Just see what you get and if you're still bored, then you can change it back."

"Or dump the whole idea." Maybe she'd go speed dating

instead. Five minutes with a guy. Even she could manage that.

"Are you all set for Sunday?" Kim asked.

She groaned. She'd been doing her best to forget about Sunday. "How could you let me agree to that? Why didn't you stop me? Or at least stop me drinking before I got to the stage where I said I'd do it. You know I'm terrified of heights."

"It's for a good cause, and it will be fun."

"Of course it will." She pushed Sunday to the back of her mind. She'd agreed to do it, but that didn't mean she had to think about it. "Right, work. I've got to find Dave the most horrible job I can for being such a tattletale."

Half an hour later the phone on the desk rang. It was Jake's assistant. "There's a call for you, a Mr. McCabe."

She hated the little zing of excitement that flashed through her at the name. She swallowed, breathed in, breathed out. "Put him through," she said.

"Jessica?" The zing fizzled to nothing as she recognized the voice. Rory McCabe.

"Yes."

"I'm calling to ask you to reconsider."

She frowned. "There's nothing to reconsider. Your son does not want our protection. There's nothing I can do."

"There's been another attempt on his life."

Shock slammed her in the stomach. She swallowed her fear. "Is he okay?"

"Fine, a few cuts and bruises. It was a letter bomb, sent to his apartment. Something went wrong and it exploded without being opened, early this morning. Destroyed the apartment, but luckily Declan was just arriving home. He was getting out of the elevator when it happened."

And where was Declan coming back from so early in the morning? She took a deep breath. "I still don't see what we can do if he refuses protection."

"He's agreed to meet with you again."

Something unidentifiable squirmed in her belly. "Maybe another company? We can recommend someone almost as good."

"No. He made it clear, it has to be you."

Why? She'd thought they'd said everything there was to say. She'd told him she hated him—got it out of her system. He'd told her she was…nice. What more was there to add? "Give me a moment." She sat back in her seat and gnawed on her lower lip, still tender from Declan's kisses. As she pondered, the door opened and Jake strolled in. He quirked one brow when he saw her on the phone, then picked up his wife and sat down with her on his lap. Jess swiveled her chair so she didn't have to watch.

What if she didn't do this and Declan died? And why was that anything to do with her? It would be his fault. He was the one being an asshole here. There were loads of companies who could guard him. He didn't have to insist on hers.

But she knew that if he was killed, she wouldn't forgive herself. However much she hated him, she didn't want him dead.

"Shit." She took a deep breath. "Where do you want to meet?"

"At the club. One o'clock. We can discuss it over lunch."

How civilized. As she opened her mouth to make a sarcastic comment, she caught Jake's eye across the desk and snapped it closed again. "I'll see you there, Mr. McCabe."

"I'll tell the door to let you in." Rory McCabe sounded amused. Wanker. She slammed the phone down before she could say anything she might regret.

"You have a tattoo?" Jake asked.

"Piss off."

He grinned. "So what's happening?"

"Obviously, I impressed Mr. McCabe with my superb client skills and my super-nice personality. The job is back on." She pushed herself to her feet. "I think I might go order my new desk."

"I'm impressed. From what Dave said I got the idea things didn't go well."

"Well, he was pretty determined that he didn't need protection. Totally deluded—it was obvious he had no chance. So, I went back alone. We talked things through. Clearly I made an impression."

For a few seconds something flickered in Jake's eyes. Suspicion perhaps? Was he doubting her people skills? Probably. He wasn't blind or stupid. She kept her expression bland. Finally, he shrugged. "Good, just keep Declan McCabe happy and alive. Avoid telling him he's an asshole, and you have the job."

Kim sat up straight on his lap. "*Declan* McCabe?" Her gaze flicked to Jess's bottom and her eyebrows rose.

Time to make a strategic exit. "Okay, gotta go. We'll catch up later."

She had about three hours and she was going to dig up everything she could on Declan and his father. Then she'd have one more meeting and decide whether she really gave a crap if Declan McCabe lived or died.

Chapter Six

Declan rubbed a finger over the cut on his forehead.

Someone had tried to blow him up.

That pissed him off more than the bullet.

He took a deep gulp of scotch, then slammed the glass down on his desk so the liquid sloshed over the sides. If he'd arrived home even moments earlier, he'd be dead, or at the least a little charred. The whole death-threat thing hadn't seemed real, even after the shooting, but now it was sinking in. Someone wanted him dead.

He tried to analyze his feelings. Not fear so much as irritation. Okay, maybe a little fear—truth was he didn't want to die. He closed his eyes and had a flashback to the moment he'd plunged into Jess's hot, tight body yesterday. And knew he would have her again. He just wasn't sure how. She hated him.

Grunt nudged at his knee from under the table, and he reached down and stroked the dog's silky head. Grunt had saved his life—he'd been just getting back from walking the dog when the letter bomb had gone off. The concierge had delivered it the previous evening and it had sat innocently on the sideboard in his apartment hallway overnight. Grunt must have sensed something amiss—as the elevator doors opened, he'd whined, pulled back, then all hell broke loose.

The police were examining the bomb now. Apparently, something had gone wrong and triggered it early. So someone incompetent was trying to kill him. That was maybe even worse.

He'd been trying to work, but couldn't settle and in the end he gave up. It was nearly time for the meeting with the security company, anyway. Jess. Heat coiled in his belly at the thought of her.

He'd gotten lucky today, but how long would that last? He hated to admit it, but his father was right; he needed some protection. He'd given in and told him to arrange a meeting. But he was sure of one thing: any protection he accepted would not include Jessica.

And it wasn't because he didn't believe she could do it. He'd gotten the background report on her and it was seriously impressive. She was UK champion in unarmed combat, whatever that involved. She'd competed in the Olympics for shooting and won a medal. No, he was sure she was competent and while she said she hated him, he was also sure that she wouldn't let that influence her doing her job.

That was all irrelevant, because no way was she putting herself in danger to protect him. Just the thought of Jess stepping in front of a bullet meant for him made him reach for the scotch.

Never going to happen.

He'd have to find another way to get her to come to him. Because he wasn't letting her disappear from his life. Not yet.

He'd woken that morning with a sense of anticipation he hadn't experienced in years. He felt vital, alive, and randy as hell. Yesterday had only whetted his appetite for more.

Obviously all those years ago, he'd walked away from her before their somewhat explosive relationship had run its course. They'd been so volatile, always arguing, fighting, making love. It had been the best sex ever, before or after, but he'd pushed that to the back of his mind. It had only taken one meeting to make him realize that he'd never forgotten her.

She was unfinished business. And he meant to finish it. And enjoy the process. And she would, too. Though he'd have to wait until his little problem was fixed, no way was she being anywhere near him while some asshole was trying to blow him up. Afterward, when it was over, he would find a way to reel her in. Once in his presence he was pretty sure she wouldn't be able to resist. The reeling in was going to be the hard part.

He relaxed back in his chair and sipped his scotch, a smile tugging at his lips just as the door opened and his father stepped into the room, Paul behind him.

"Why the hell are you looking so cheerful?" his dad said, throwing himself onto the leather sofa. "Didn't someone just try to blow you up? And why are you drinking at eleven in the morning. You never drink in the office."

He raised his glass. "Just celebrating being alive."

"Hmm." His father didn't look convinced. "Well, I came to tell you that the problem is sorted."

"It is?"

"I told you I could sort it out. You should have let me do that from the start, and then you wouldn't have gotten in this mess."

"You were the one who wanted the company respectable," Declan pointed out. "That means leave the criminals to the police. So who was it?"

"You don't need to know, but I pulled in a few favors and they won't be bothering you again."

"And they admitted it?"

"Well, the shooting they did, though they wouldn't own up to the bombing—probably some overambitious underling wanting to impress his boss and taking things into his own hands. But the bottom line is they're not coming after you. We can cancel your babysitters."

Declan sat back and considered the information. Yeah, it would be good to get back to normal. Or would it? "Normal" hadn't been that great; in fact it had been bloody boring. The last couple of days, he'd actually felt alive. There was something wrong with his reasoning, but he still couldn't deny it.

"You don't look too pleased," his dad said.

He gave himself a mental shake. "No, I am."

"Good. Well, I'll call up and cancel the meeting with the security company."

Which meant no Jess for lunch. He couldn't believe the stab of disappointment right to his gut at the thought.

It occurred to him that now there was no danger, there was no reason to keep her at a safe distance. Problem with that logic was, that with no danger there was also no reason for her to come anywhere near him.

"Don't cancel the meeting."

"What?" His father had been on the point of rising. Now he sank back down.

"I think I'll feel safer with some protection for a little while." Declan rubbed his arm over the bandage. "Just until we're sure I'm in the clear. You said it yourself, they didn't admit to the bombing. What if that overambitious underling decides to try again?"

"Oh, I'm sure these people are capable of keeping their underlings in control." He studied Declan through narrowed eyes. "Could this be anything to do with your ex-girlfriend? I heard she spent a rather long time in your office yesterday."

Declan glanced at Paul, who was standing by the window hands in his pockets. He didn't say anything. Declan had always known he was his father's man but for the first time he didn't like the idea he had a spy in his territory. Maybe it was time to get another assistant.

"We were just talking about old times."

"Why do I find that hard to believe?" His dad shrugged. "We've got the money. If you want to play some sort of game with your little ex, who am I to argue?" He gave Declan one last look and rose to his feet. "By the way, your mother is coming over for my birthday in a couple of weeks."

"She is?" That was a first.

"Yes, and she's bringing Penny with her."

"What? Why the hell would she do that?"

"I invited her," he said, then hesitated a moment before continuing, "I'm worried about you."

"And how does inviting my ex-fiancé to your birthday make me any safer?" Maybe he should lay off the scotch.

"I don't mean the case." His dad shifted from foot to foot as though uncomfortable. "You need a life outside the business."

"I'm fine," he ground out.

"You're far from fine. You're a goddamn robot, Declan."

His jaw clenched. He'd done everything the family wanted of him and this was what they thought of him? Something occurred to him then. "Is that why you threw Jessica at me?"

"Maybe."

Declan shook his head. "The scourge of the East End of London turned matchmaker." It seemed inconceivable.

At the door his father turned back. "But it worked. It's good to finally see some sign that you're actually human, even if it has taken a bullet and a bomb. Your mother will be pleased. I'll see you at the club."

"Okay. I'm going to check into the hotel first, get Grunt settled." His apartment had been trashed. The damage from the explosion had been relatively small, but a fire had broken out and the smoke damage was extensive.

As the door closed behind them Declan poured himself another scotch, sat back in his chair, and considered the conversation. What the bloody hell did his mother have to do with it?

• • •

Jess had a certain sense of déjà vu as the taxi deposited them outside the nightclub. This was where she'd had that final showdown with Rory McCabe all those years ago.

The place was closed, but Dave tapped on the door, and it opened within seconds. A man stood there. He was huge, a slab of steroid-induced muscle, his black T-shirt stretched tight over bulging chest. One of Rory's bouncers. He looked

0. 0. 000

over them briefly and then stood aside to let them in.

They followed him through into the main area with the large dance floor and podiums scattered about. She'd danced on one of those podiums the night she'd met Declan. The place hadn't changed at all, though it appeared different in daylight, the blinds open.

They passed the table where she'd had her last confrontation with Rory McCabe, but they didn't pause. Instead, they followed the man through a door in the far wall and into a private area with a table set for lunch. Three places.

Rory McCabe was seated at one of them, facing the door. He looked so like his son that a shiver ran down her spine. She would do well to remember the relationship. Rory was a hard-nosed bastard, and while Declan had a veneer of civilization, underneath she was guessing he was just the same. From her research, she had learned that the business was totally legit, but no one was that successful without a ruthless streak. Rory rose to his feet as they entered, his lips twitching as he caught sight of Dave and Steve behind her. "You brought your own bodyguards. I assure you, you're quite safe here."

She ignored the comment. "This is Dave Grantham and Steve Forrest. They'll be working on Declan's team if we take the job."

He nodded and spoke to the young man who'd led them here. "Could you set the table for two more and inform the kitchen."

She gave her best insincere smile. "I hope we haven't inconvenienced you."

"Why do I get the impression you don't give a damn if I'm inconvenienced?"

She didn't answer, just shrugged and stepped aside as the young man pulled up two extra chairs and repositioned the others. She took one, leaving a gap between her and Rory. Steve hesitated a second, then took that seat, and Dave took the one on her other side. Maybe they'd sensed some animosity between her and the older man.

"Drinks?" Rory asked waving a hand at his own glass of scotch. "I remember you had a thing about my malt scotch."

No way was she touching the stuff today. She wanted a clear head. "Water will be fine."

Rory raised an eyebrow but took his seat and studied her. "You're not at all what I expected you to become."

"Really?" She kept her tone disinterested. She had a good idea what he'd expected her to become. He'd made that clear at their last meeting.

"Actually, I like the scar." He gave a small smile. "Gives you character."

She smiled sweetly; she'd been practicing. "That's nice. I aim to please."

Beside her, Steve choked on a mouthful of water, and she reached across and patted him on the back.

Rory's eyes narrowed on the movement. "So," he said, "I hear you went back to see Declan yesterday and I know you stayed for a while."

He didn't sound too bothered by the idea. Had she suddenly become acceptable? "Still spying on him?"

Before he could answer, the door opened and Declan stepped through. He closed the door behind him and stood just inside the room, taking in the occupants. Like yesterday, he was immaculately dressed in a dark suit and tie, his hair in place. The only sign of his close encounter with death was a cut on his forehead.

Staring at the jagged red line, the fact sank in: he could have died that morning. The idea made her want to lock him away somewhere safe until all this was sorted. And she couldn't understand the reaction.

Declan nodded at Dave and Steve, ignored his father, and finally focused on Jess. His gaze dropped to her mouth and he stared.

. . .

Once again, she wasn't wearing any makeup but her lips were pink, maybe a little swollen from his kisses yesterday. Her dark blue eyes held no expression.

There was a seat opposite her, but first he went and grabbed the bottle of scotch and a glass from the sideboard behind his father. He took it to the table and sat down, poured himself a drink, and swallowed it in one go. He looked up to find everyone watching him with varying expressions, from Jess's deadpan, to the two men's disapproval, to his father's…amusement?

"Was the hotel okay?" his dad asked.

"It was fine."

"You could always come and stay with me."

"I don't think so."

His father cast a glance at Jess. "Worried I'll cramp your style?"

"No. Anyway, it's only for one night. Paul's finding me an apartment to rent. One I can move into immediately."

Jess cleared her throat. Loudly. "Er…do you think we can move on here?"

He sat back in his chair and smiled. "Of course."

"So have you changed your mind? Is the job on?"

He held her gaze. "The job is on." He tried to read her expression, but she was giving nothing away. Back when she was seventeen, he'd been able to read her every thought. She'd hidden nothing, flashed every emotion for everyone to see. Somewhere along the way she'd learned to hide that and he felt a flicker of sadness. She'd been so full of life, fizzing with energy. Like a wild fire, liable to go out of control at any moment.

That last meeting, at the hospital, she'd been full of disbelief. He'd told her they could still be friends and that she should come to him if she needed anything. But he'd had to go, had to get some distance. She turned him into a person he didn't want to be. The close encounter with the police had shown him that. The police hated his family—and maybe they'd had good reason. His older brother Logan, had already been serving time on some trumped-up assault charge that anyone else would have walked away from.

A week before the crash, she'd stolen a goddamn car. And he'd gone a long with her, because she loved the thrill of danger.

And so did he. He'd just buried it deep.

She'd brought him face to face with a side of himself that he'd always kept under rigid control. A side that at eighteen had craved walking on the wild side. And that was why he'd had to leave.

"Why?" she asked.

"Because I've accepted I need professional help." He shrugged. "I thought the shooting was maybe a one-off that they wanted to make a point. Scare me a little."

"And now?"

"Now I think they want me dead."

She raised a brow, opened her mouth, but at that moment the door opened and a waitress wheeled in a trolley with lunch. They were all quiet as she served them, filling glasses with white wine and placing plates of lobster-tail salad in front of each of them. He wasn't hungry and ignored the food, instead poured himself another glass of scotch. He sat back and sipped it, watching her.

The men all tucked into the food, but Jess picked up her fork and then placed it down again. "Why us?" she asked.

"Your company has an excellent reputation."

"So do a lot of companies."

"Okay, because I know you and trust you."

"Really?" She definitely sounded skeptical. Relaxing back, she rubbed a finger over her plump lower lip while she considered him.

She was wearing another black pantsuit that looked identical to yesterday's and a white shirt. Maybe she bought her clothes in bulk. Her jacket was buttoned up tight, but he could see the faint bulge of a shoulder holster beneath the material. She was armed and dangerous. His lips curled at the thought.

"Something funny?" she asked, her tone mild.

"Not at all. I was just wondering if you're always armed."

"Of course not. Just when I think a gun might come in handy."

The look she gave him made it clear just what use she would like to put the gun to.

"So you'll accept the job?" his dad asked, putting down his knife and fork and taking a sip of wine. The others hadn't touched theirs, but maybe they already considered themselves on duty.

He held his breath while he waited for her answer, though he knew it would be yes. However cool she was pretending to be, she wasn't immune to him. Yesterday, she'd come apart in his arms. He had a flashback to her, hot, wet, clenching around his dick, and twitched in his pants.

"Yes, providing your son agrees to follow our advice."

"Of course," he murmured. "Within reason."

"What would you consider unreasonable?"

"I refuse to hide away. I refuse to let these bastards dictate what I can and can't do. Where I go."

She pursed her lips. "Fair enough."

"Money is no object," his father put in.

"That's good to know. So," she said sounding brisk and businesslike, "I'll coordinate the job, but Dave and Steve will be responsible for the team and one of them will be on duty at all time. You haven't met Steve." She turned to the man at her side. He was tall, dark-haired, good-looking and she smiled at him, then rested a hand on his arm in a familiar way. Declan's gaze fixed on the gesture, his jaw tightening. Only the fact that the man's eyes widened a fraction saved him.

Jess was trying to wind him up. Trying to make him believe there was something more than a professional relationship between the two of them.

"I don't think so," he said. "I want you on the team. I want you protecting me."

"Why?"

"I told you, I trust you. But also there are situations where a male bodyguard might be inconvenient. I have some sensitive meetings coming up, business dinners. You'll be less confrontational."

Dave snorted in disbelief. Obviously, it wasn't only with him that she was hostile.

"Okay, *appear* less confrontational." For a minute, he thought she would argue, but then she gave an abrupt nod.

"Okay, you'll have to provide us with your schedule. Mark on it any situations where you think the guys will be too…confrontational and I'll see if I can fit them in."

"Good of you."

"Yes, it is." She rose to her feet. "Now, if you'll excuse me for a minute, I must go visit the ladies' room. Why don't you start working on that schedule with the guys?"

• • •

Jess took a deep breath. What she actually needed was some fresh air. Her skin was flushed and she felt as though the walls were closing in on her. She hurried from the room, ignoring the sensation of his eyes following her every move.

Ever since he'd entered the room, she'd had to fight back the memories of them together. His hard body pressing her back against the wall, his hard cock filling her. She hoped he wasn't going to have this effect on her all the time or it would make working with him a little…

She exhaled loudly as the door closed behind her. She suspected Declan was quite aware of the effect he had on her and was expecting a repeat performance. Maybe that was the real reason he had asked for her to be added to the bodyguard detail. What she needed to understand was why she had said yes.

Or was she deluding herself. Again. Would she take the first opportunity to shag him mindless? All in the name of putting the past behind her.

She headed across the main room and through a door into the corridor that held the ladies' room, but she walked straight past to a second door at the end of the hallway. As she pushed it open, a waft of cool air brushed over her cheeks. There was a hint of rain in the air, misting her skin. The door led into an alley that ran alongside the building and opened up thirty feet away onto the main street. Traffic rumbled in the distance as she let herself out. Leaning against the brick wall, she opened her jacket and ran a hand around the back of her neck. Her skin was clammy, and strands of her long ponytail clung to her neck. Maybe she should have it all cut off. In the army she'd kept it short but hadn't had it cut since, except when she attacked it with a pair of nail scissors if the split ends got too bad.

Declan had loved her long hair. Yeah, maybe it was time for a cut.

As though she had conjured him up with a thought, he stepped out of the door into the alley. Unsurprised, she realized she'd been expecting him in a weird, subconscious sort of way.

He came to a halt directly in front of her, his gaze fixed on her face. "I thought we should talk. I'm sure we both have questions."

"Maybe we should." She tilted her head and returned his scrutiny. Her heart hitched; he was so beautiful, just looking at him started an ache in her chest. She pushed the feeling aside. He was right; she had questions. "I'll go first. Why did your father throw the two of us together?"

His lips curved in a small smile. "He's matchmaking."

"What?" She shook her head. "But he hates me."

"Desperate times call for desperate measures. He thinks I'm a robot and need to get a life outside the business. He's been dangling just about every fuckable woman in London under my nose since I got here. Today he came right out and admitted it."

She didn't like the thought of that. "And did you…fuck any of them I mean?"

He grinned. "Only you."

Shit, she shouldn't like that, but it made her feel all warm and fuzzy.

"My turn," he said. "Why did you really come back yesterday? Why take this job?"

She sighed and tugged on her ponytail. "You already know. I told you, I want to move on, and right now you seem to be a stumbling block. So I'm facing up to my issues. Head-on. If you'd stayed, I would no doubt have realized you were a prick back then and dumped you myself. But you walked away. I'll never forgive you, but I want to forget you."

His lips tightened for a second, and then he shrugged. "Fair enough."

"Plus, I really do have to prove myself with this job if I want my promotion."

"So, we spend some time together, hopefully my dad will back off the matchmaking, you'll get me out of your system, and you'll do it so nicely that you'll get a promotion."

"It's a win-win situation," she said. At least in theory.

He swiped his tongue over his lower lip and regarded her for long seconds. "You know I want you?"

She gave a jerky nod.

"And are you going to let me have you. Is that part of the deal? It's really the only way you'll get me out of your system. I suggest we fuck often and long until we're both sated and you can crawl away."

He took a step closer, and her every nerve went on alert, her skin tingling. Part of her hated that he made her feel so alive, but at the same time she reveled in the sensations. There was a sense of inevitability as his head lowered to hers and he took her mouth in a deep, wet kiss. She opened beneath him and his tongue pushed inside, filling her. He tasted of scotch, and the smoky flavor invoked memories that heated her body. Without thinking, she raised her hands, her fingers sinking in the short silky hair at the back of his neck and holding him against her. He deepened the kiss, so she thought he might devour her, pushing her back against the rough wall, his body hard, his erection obvious. He was breathing fast as he raised his head and stared down into her face.

"Tell me you weren't sitting at that table, remembering the feel of my cock inside you." He emphasized the words with a shift of his hips, pushing against her belly so a pulse started between her thighs, and she pressed up against him, unable to stop the movement.

It started to rain, the drops almost hissing against her heated skin. She didn't want to think anymore, and she pulled him down to her. He buried his face in the curve of her neck, his teeth nipping the skin where her shoulder met her throat, then soothing the bite with slow strokes of his tongue.

"You wanted me to be jealous in there. Maybe I need to mark you as mine." He sucked the skin of her throat between his lips. He was giving her a goddamned love bite and she couldn't stir herself to do anything about it. Hell, she liked it.

"You always loved fucking outside. Anywhere and everywhere."

"You didn't," she said. He'd liked to make love in bed, where he could take his time. But she had loved the added edge, the fear of being found. Now that didn't factor into it at all, she just loved the feel of his mouth on her skin, his big hands tugging her shirt out of her pants, his palm hot against her belly, smoothing up over the sensitive skin, then cupping one breast in his palm, rubbing over the nipple. He reached between them with his other hand, flicking open the buttons so the material parted. Leaning back slightly, his hand slipped inside her bra to free one breast. He took the nipple into his mouth and suckled hard so flashes of pleasure shot to her groin, flooding her sex. He nipped with his teeth while his knee rode up between her thighs, pushing against her core.

The sensations were spiraling inside her, and she didn't protest as his hand pushed inside her pants, down beneath the cotton of her panties.

"Christ, you're wet. You want to come, baby. Here, outside, while your friends wait for you?"

She didn't care. She needed this. She rested her head back against the wall, eyes closed, the rain falling on her upturned face as one finger pushed inside, then spread the moisture up over her clit. As he found the tight, swollen nub, she let out a gasp. He rubbed over it with his hard finger, massaging, as the pleasure built.

"You like? Next time I'm going to kiss you here, suck you and lick you until you come all over my face." His murmured words, and the image they evoked, tipped her over the edge, and she came hard, pushing against his hand. He pinched her clit, and her knees nearly gave way as she came again.

Finally, he withdrew his hand. Her lids flickered and she found him watching her, beads of moisture glistening on his skin. He raised his hand to his mouth, licked his fingers, and she nearly came again.

"Holy shit," she muttered.

"Yeah. Well, one of us is sorted. My turn now." He reached out, took her hand where it hung limp at her side, and pressed it against his groin. He was hard, huge, pressing against his fly. A car passed the end of the alley, and she had a moment of awareness as to where they were. Down an alley, in central London, in broad daylight. But before sanity could totally take over, she tightened her hand around him through the soft material and he groaned. She loved the sound.

She rubbed up and down the length of his shaft, then hesitated, her fingers on the fastener, just a moment.

"Come on, Jess, you're killing me here." She'd always loved the power she had over him, how she could make him beg. Outside of sex, he'd always been the one in control. But in these moments, he'd been hers.

She flicked open the button, put her hands to the zipper—

"Jess?" The voice came from inside the building, and she went still.

"Fuck," Declan cursed under his breath. He looked around as if there was someplace to disappear, but apart from the main street there was nowhere. "I don't suppose you'd tell them to piss off?" he asked.

Jess shook her head; she didn't trust herself to speak

just then. She took a shaky step back and glanced down at herself. Her jacket and shirt were open, her breasts spilling out of the white cotton bra. She shoved herself back in, wincing as her sensitive nipples scraped across the material, then dragged her shirt together and fastened the buttons, tucked the ends into her waistband and was decent as the door opened.

She cast a quick look at Declan. He was leaning, one shoulder against the wall, ignoring the now steady rain, his legs crossed at the ankles.

Dave stepped through the door, eying up the two of them, although they were nowhere even close to each other. "We're ready to go."

"Good." Her voice sounded firm. At least she thought it had, but Dave's brows drew together.

"You okay? Do we have a problem?"

"No problem."

Declan pushed himself away from the wall and faced the other man. "We were just ironing out the finer details of Jess's role."

"Really?"

Steve entered the alley behind Dave. "You found her then?"

"As you see." Dave waved a hand in her direction, and she got the distinct impression he wasn't happy. Maybe it was the tic in his cheek.

"Well, I'll let you go then," Declan said. "I'll be at my office if you need me."

"You're not going anywhere yet," Dave said. "We have another man on his way. He'll be on duty with Steve until we get the roster organized. But until he gets here, you stay put."

For a moment, she thought he was going to tell Dave to bugger off. Then he glanced at her and shrugged. "Okay." He turned to Steve. "Let me know when you're ready to leave."

Steve nodded but didn't speak.

As he passed her, Declan leaned in close. "You owe me, baby girl. And I'll be collecting."

Chapter Seven

She'd thought she'd gotten away with it. Dave said nothing as the taxi took them back to the office. But as the entered the building, he steered her into one of the small conference rooms they used for meeting clients.

"You have a hickey," he said, his tone tinged with disgust. He shook his head. "How the fucking mighty have fallen. The 'Ice Queen' giving it out in an alley in broad daylight in the middle of London."

"We were just...talking about old times. No big deal." She sat herself down on one of the upright chairs around the table, rested her chin in her hand, and waited for Dave to get over it.

"No big deal? Really? Because I'm guessing Declan McCabe is the reason no one has won that pool we've got going in the office."

She ignored the comment, but she wasn't being totally fair. This was a dangerous business, and Dave had a right to know what was going on and to worry that she would compromise the job. She'd hardly behaved in a professional manner. But shit, surely everyone was allowed to have a bad day.

Though "bad" really didn't describe it. Declan's hands had felt so *good*. Why did her own never feel that way? For that matter, why did no other man's? Was she doomed to find only him a turn-on? Maybe she'd been programmed too young. Now her body could only respond to one man. Crap.

"Earth to Jess."

Dave waved a hand in front of her, and she snapped out of her daydream.

"Sorry," she muttered, sitting up straight.

"So you should be. You left us with that asshole. I don't like him. He's got an agenda."

"Rory McCabe?" No, she didn't like him either. And yeah, he was up to something. But matchmaking? It hardly seemed likely. And certainly not between her and Declan.

"Why is he pushing this?" Dave asked. "Why us?"

"I don't know. That's the honest-to-God truth. I'm as much in the dark as you are."

"But you still plan to take the job?" He stopped pacing and took the seat next to her, dragging it around so he could stare into her face. "Look, I've known you a long time. I've fought beside you. Christ, you've covered my back a dozen times. You're the toughest woman I've ever come across, and I would have sworn nothing could get through that armor."

"So?" She gave a casual shrug. "Nothing's changed."

He raked a hand through his hair, pressed his fingers to his forehead. "Like fuck it hasn't. You've got a goddamned hickey. The pair of you were making out like a couple of randy fucking teenagers." She looked away and he sighed. "All I'm saying is we can still walk away from this one."

"We've agreed to do the job."

"Then persuade me that we aren't making a big mistake."

She hated justifying herself, but Dave deserved this. "Do you believe the threat is real? Does Declan need protecting?"

Dave nodded. "Yeah. No doubt."

"And can we provide that protection."

"*We* can. I'm not so sure about you, and I don't like the fact that he's insisting you're part of the team. And I like it even less that you're caving in to that."

"I'm hardly caving in. I'm just going along with it for my own reasons."

"Will those reasons compromise the job?"

She tugged on her ponytail as she considered her answer. Declan, whether she liked it or not, had the ability to make her lose all sense of where she was, of everything except who she was with, and what he was making her feel. Not good for a bodyguard. She was hardly going to be able to protect him if she was underneath him or on top or… But although she was shaken by the strength of her feelings, she had to see this through. Or she would never be free of him. Maybe as he'd said they should sate themselves on each other, and once sated, she'd dump his sorry ass and never look back.

"Okay, so here's the thing. We'll work out a schedule and I'll be on it, but not on it. We make sure I have back up at all times. Rory can pay."

Had she made a mistake letting Declan back in her life?

The question refused to be banished as she lay in bed that night, staring at the ceiling, unable to sleep.

But there was no reason why he should be a problem as long as she kept her wits about her.

He was strictly business. Well sort of.

Her hand went to her throat, and she stroked the mark he had left. What did he want from her? Protection against his dad's matchmaking schemes? She just couldn't buy into that one.

Sex?

More likely. Maybe like her, he felt they were unfinished business and if they shagged enough, they would eventually be finished and the craving would fade away.

Or did he want something else?

Maybe the next few days would clear things up.

Right now, she needed sleep, but she twitched and turned and if she closed her eyes, all she could see was Declan.

The phone rang on her bedside table and she jumped. It was close to midnight. Who the hell would call her now? Unless there had been some sort of disaster at work.

She picked it up, but didn't recognize the number. "Hello?"

"Where the hell are you?"

She recognized the voice instantly. "Steve? Is that you, darling?"

"No, it fucking isn't and don't pretend you don't know exactly who this is."

"Declan, what the hell do you want? There had better be someone trying to kill you right now, and they'd better have taken down both of the very capable guards I sent to babysit you."

"I told you I wanted *you*. That was the deal."

"And you'll get me. Just not 24-7. Where are your guards?" she asked, suddenly suspicious.

"Don't worry. They're in the next room. I'm safe, but it's nice to know you care."

"I don't. But if you die, I don't get my promotion. Furthermore, the company has never lost a client yet. I'd rather not start now. It's bad for business."

"Sweet. So where are you?"

"It's midnight. I'm in bed."

"Naked?"

"No, not naked."

"Could you get naked?" His voice sank lower and warmth washed through her. Just the sound of his voice sent tremors skittering across her skin. Why him? Why did he have to be the one to bring her body to life?

He'd made no indication that he wanted anything more from her than sex. And she was good with that. She would never trust any man with her heart again. Least of all this one, after he'd done such a great job of shattering it the first time. The experience had taken something from her, something fragile that she guessed would never come back: trust.

"Jess? You're thinking too much. You know you want me. Need me."

"Want maybe. Need...no. And you know why?"

"Tell me."

She reached across to her bedside cabinet and picked up her vibrator. "Because I've got something much better, right next to me."

"You have?"

"Yeah, it's long and it's hard and it doesn't have a mouth

so no chance it's going to say something that will piss me off."

"You like my mouth. You always liked what I did with my mouth."

"I don't remember."

"Come on over, and I'll remind you." His words made the heat pool in her belly and warm wetness soak her sex. Because she did remember. She'd never been able to get enough of his mouth on her. And he'd seemed the same. He'd spent hours tasting her, licking, devouring. She bit back a moan.

"You remembering yet?" he murmured down the phone. "I particularly recall how you used to love it when I—"

She clicked on the vibrator and held it close to the phone. It was quiet on the other end for a whole minute. Then she heard a deep sigh.

"Christ, I wish I was there. You got a camera on that phone?"

"Not a hope in hell."

"My dick is so fucking hard. Has been since you walked out on me this afternoon." His breathing was loud. "Tell me what you're doing, Jess? Tell me how you pleasure yourself. Are you wet? Touch yourself."

She swallowed. But holy shit this was hot. She imagined Declan in his hotel room, sprawled on a big bed. The phone in one hand... "You first."

"Sweetheart, my hand is around my cock. I wish it was you, but if I don't get off soon, I'll explode. Go on, talk to me...tell me what you're doing. Stroke your breasts."

She closed her eyes for a second, then took a deep breath. Jamming the phone in the crook between her neck and her shoulder, she slipped her free hand beneath her tank top and stroked her palm over the peak, imagined Declan's dark head there, kissing her, his lips tugging on the nipples. She pinched one between her thumb and her finger and moaned.

"You doing it, baby?"

"Oh yeah."

"Now lower. Touch yourself. Tell me how wet you are."

She stroked her hand over her belly, then down under the drawstring of her pants. Her whole body quivered in anticipation. It had never felt like this before. Her fingers slid through the folds, gliding across her drenched sex.

"Talk to me, baby."

"I'm wet."

"Wet enough to push that vibrator inside?"

She wriggled out of her pants, the vibrator buzzing in her hand. "It's sliding inside, Declan." She pressed the head against her opening and pushed it inside, the vibrations tingling through her body. "And it feels so damn good."

"My cock would feel better. I need to picture this—describe it to me."

"It's a rabbit, and the little ears are tickling me. Oh God." She closed her eyes and it was Declan's fingers between her legs, his cock deep inside her. She pulled the vibrator out and pushed back again, harder this time, then left it lodged inside, the pleasure building, a heavy weight in her belly, swelling and spreading outward.

"What's happening?" he asked.

"I'm going to come in about ten seconds."

"We'll come together."

An image of Declan, his fingers wrapped around his own cock, pumping into his fist, filled her mind. The sensations became too much, and she crashed over the edge, getting no relief as the vibrations continued, and she came again. She fumbled between her thighs, switched off the vibrator, and collapsed back on the pillows. She'd dropped the phone; it lay on the bed and she picked it up with a trembling hand. She licked her lips, swallowed, finally, managed to speak. "You still here?"

"Oh yeah. That was sexy, baby, but next time I want to be there."

"Never going to happen. Good night, Declan."

• • •

His father had once told him that everyone made mistakes. It was how you dealt with them that showed what you were made of. And what you learned from them. A man who made the same mistakes time and time again was…

Desperate.

Shit, he couldn't believe they had indulged in phone sex last night. God, he'd been turned on. Almost as turned on as having her up against the wall in his office, or feeling her come apart for him in that alley, her hot, slick muscles, clamping on his finger.

Jess had always been his one big mistake. He'd known from the moment he set eyes on her, in that tiny little scrap of a black dress, sitting at his father's table in the nightclub, that she was trouble. Big trouble. She'd been swilling champagne and fluttering her eyelashes at his goddamn father.

He'd put a stop to that.

Even back then Rory McCabe had been going straight, and news that a seventeen-year-old was underage drinking in his club was guaranteed to piss him off. The police were always looking for an excuse to close him down. Any slight step out of line and they would throw the book at him.

Declan had recognized Jess from school, although she was a year younger than him. She was seriously beautiful, impossible to miss. And he'd been eighteen. Horny as only a teenager could be. What was his excuse this time around?

The apartment took up the whole top floor of the building. Paul had apparently run the possibilities past Jess yesterday afternoon, and this was the most suitable, the easiest to keep him safe.

"Come on, boy." He tugged on Grunt's lead and the dog followed him reluctantly into the elevator. Grunt didn't like new places—they brought his many insecurities to the fore—and Declan leaned down and stroked the animal's big head.

Grunt had adopted him soon after Declan had moved to the city. He'd found him injured and emaciated in the alley alongside his apartment building and taken him to the vet, got him fixed up, and Grunt had moved in. He'd never had a pet growing up. He'd spent too much time moving between continents for it to be viable.

The elevator opened into a big marble-floored foyer with a multitude of doors leading off. He'd left his body-guard in the reception area and been told that there was a replacement up here, but the place appeared deserted.

He took a step farther into the room, Grunt's claws clicking on the marble as the door opposite opened and Jess stood in the doorway. She looked exactly as she had on the previous two meetings. Black suit, white shirt, no makeup, hair pulled into a ponytail. He'd sort of hoped she would have made an obvious effort, tried to impress him, but nothing. Not that she needed makeup or fancy clothes. Just that his ego was getting a bashing. As his gaze dropped down over her body, he had a flashback to the sound of her panted breaths over the phone last night and his dick pulsed.

"Morning," she said, her face completely blank of expression. Then her gaze dropped to the dog at his side and he saw the first genuine smile since they'd met again two days ago. He hadn't known she liked dogs.

She strode across the floor and sank down on her haunches. "Is he okay with strangers?"

"Yes. Though he's not very obedient."

"I'll send my friend Dani over. She's a dog trainer. She'll get him sorted in no time."

She reached out and stroked Grunt's head, then scratched under his chin. And he felt a flicker of some emotion. He was jealous of his dog. Just because Jess was being nice to Grunt. But he didn't want Jess to be nice to *him*. All he wanted from her was sex and then good-bye.

Didn't he?

"What is he?" she asked.

He shook himself. "I'm not sure. A bit of German shepherd, a bit of pit bull, a bit of Great Dane."

"A lot of Great Dane," she replied with a laugh and something twisted inside him, flooding his mind with memories. Back when he'd first known her, she'd laughed all the time. What had changed her? She'd joined up only months after he'd left. He'd seen her service records; she'd done three tours in Afghanistan, probably enough to turn anyone serious. But why had she gone that route in the first place?

"I didn't know you liked dogs."

"You don't know a lot about me. Then again, why should you? We had a fling when we were both little more than kids. There's nothing else between us, and you don't need to know." She straightened and looked up at him. "On the other hand, I need to know all about you. Someone wants to kill you. Let's go talk about that. There's coffee on in the kitchen." Without waiting for him to answer she spun around and headed back the way she had come.

He released Grunt from his lead, but the dog stayed at his side as he followed her. A little twinge of guilt nagged at his insides that maybe he should have come clean and told her that his father believed the problem sorted. That he was in all likelihood in no danger. But he was pretty sure if he did that, she would walk out. And it wasn't as though she was overly concerned for his safety. He was clearly nothing more than a job to her.

And there was something else to consider. While she was guarding him she wasn't putting herself in danger guarding some other asshole. A shudder ran through him at the thought.

"I like your new apartment, by the way." She sat at the granite counter that ran along one side of the room, a mug of coffee in front of her. She nodded to the coffee machine behind her and he went and filled up a mug for himself. "So I've read the report," she said. "But I'd like to hear the whole thing from you."

He talked her through the events of the past few months. She stopped him now and then with questions. "You've been based in the US since college. Why the move back here?"

"My father was running the UK side of things. He collapsed last year. At first they thought it was a heart attack."

"Really? I didn't think he had a heart."

He ignored the comment and continued. He was quite aware there had been no love lost between his father and Jess. But then it had been a difficult time. His father had blamed himself for Declan's brother, Logan, being in prison and was determined the same wouldn't happen to his other son.

Jess listened but didn't speak again until he came to the part where they'd brought in the police. She obviously picked up some vibes.

"I can understand why your father doesn't like the police, but why you?"

He shrugged. "I grew up believing they weren't my friends. And they weren't. They were after my father and would have loved something on me. Even as a kid."

"You can't know that."

"They didn't make a secret of it. They harassed him, even coming to our home. My brother was put away when he was twenty-one on some trumped-up assault charge that anyone else would have walked away from with a warning."

"I didn't know you had a brother."

"Logan is my half brother. He came from my father's first marriage. But my dad had custody from when Logan was ten, so we're close."

"Then why did we never meet?"

"I told you, he was in prison when we had our…thing. But he's out now. You'll probably get to meet him if you stick around. He manages the nightclubs."

She stood up, picked up her coffee, and turned away to stare out of the window for a minute. When she turned back, her lips were pursed. "Is that why you were so upset the night I stole that car?"

"Partly. I'm also a law-abiding citizen, and I don't actually think stealing cars is something you do for kicks. But yeah. They would have thrown the book at me and smiled the whole time they were doing it."

She gave a small nod, came back, and sat down. "Okay, finish the story."

He told her everything he could think of, then sat back while she considered it.

"So," she said eventually, "you're a witness for the case?"

"Yes, though they have enough other witnesses to seal it without me."

"Then this is more in the way of retribution than saving their asses."

"Maybe. To be honest, I have no clue. This has never happened to me before."

"What? You mean no one's ever tried to kill you?" She frowned. "Hey, you're not married are you?"

He didn't like how she made the connection between someone wanting to kill him and his being married. "No."

"Fiancée?"

"No."

"Girlfriend?"

"No."

"Friendly neighborhood prostitute who pops over and relieves the pressure every now and then?"

"No." He'd been over here for just under a year now and hadn't been laid in all that time. Well until Jess. He hadn't even been on a date. And he hadn't noticed. Before that there had been Penny. "I was engaged. We broke up before I moved over here."

"Why? What was wrong with her? Didn't Rory like her?"

"Nothing was wrong with her. She was perfect, and my father loved her. She was my mother's best friend's daughter, and my mother loved her as well."

"Wow. So what went wrong between you and little Ms. Perfect?"

That was why he'd gone out with her. He'd tried the not so perfect and that had gotten him nothing but a whole load of grief. So why not try the opposite? Penny was beautiful, clever—she was a corporate lawyer—smart, sophisticated. The perfect wife. And he'd been bored out of his mind with her. The relationship had lacked any spark, but wasn't that what he'd wanted? No danger of falling for her, and no danger of crashing at the end of that fall.

"Nothing went wrong. It just didn't work out." Penny had actually ended the engagement. From the outset, she'd told him she was happy with a marriage that had more to do with convenience than with love, but in the end she had broken it off. She'd told him he wasn't the man she had first thought. That she didn't believe he would be happy with their loveless marriage. But he wasn't expecting "happy." In the end, breaking up with Penny hadn't bothered him and he supposed that proved her point. "We're still friends."

"How sweet."

"So why the interest in my love life?"

She grinned. "Or lack of it. Just considering options."

"You think you want the position?" Why the hell had he said that? "You want to be my girlfriend, Jess?"

She allowed her gaze to wander down over him. Her tongue poked out, small and pointed, swiping over her plump lower lip, and heat pooled in his belly.

"Bloody hell, no," she replied. "I have absolutely no aspirations to be your girlfriend, Declan. Been there. Done that. Have no wish to repeat the…mistake." She gave him a smile that didn't reach her midnight-blue eyes. "The sex is great, and I've no problem with a little extracurricular activity providing it doesn't interfere with the job. But be your girlfriend? I'd rather strip naked, roll myself in honey, and sit on an anthill."

"Nice visual. At least the stripping naked bit."

She ignored the comment. "But the girlfriend thing would be an ideal cover, so it's best if the position is open. It will allow me to stay close without being too obvious. And it will have the added benefit of stopping your dad's matchmaking habit. If that's what you really want."

"I want."

"But be very clear, this relationship is not real and it's totally temporary. Once the job is over, we're done. Finished. We walk away."

"Of course." Just under three weeks. Would it be enough to get her out of his system?

"Okay, I'll run it past Jake."

"Jake?"

"Jake Knight. He owns the company."

He didn't like that she was on such familiar terms with the guy. "How about you?"

She'd gotten up and placed her mug in the dishwasher. Now she turned back to him, leaning against the machine, hands in her pockets. "How about me what?"

He pushed himself to his feet and took the couple of steps that brought him directly in front of her. "Do you have a man in your life, Jess?" From this position, he could look down to the swell of her breasts beneath the white cotton shirt. Not that there was a lot to see, no cleavage on show.

"And why is that any of your business?"

"Well, I'd hate to get one lot of bad guys off my back only to piss off someone else."

"There's no one you need worry your head about."

"I thought you and that Steve guy were an item."

"Well, you thought wrong. There's nobody right now."

He liked that. But he didn't like that he liked it. God, he was fucked-up. At least where Jess was concerned. On a good note, she had said she wasn't averse to sex with him. Hardly a romantic comment, but then he didn't want romance. But he did want her. Quite desperately. In fact he couldn't remember wanting a woman quite so much since… Since more than ten years ago when he'd last slept with Jess.

But then she hadn't been a woman back then. She'd been a seventeen–year-old girl, who'd been crazy for him. He'd known that. Just as he'd known there would be nothing long-term between them. But every time he'd tried to walk away she'd pulled him back. Until the last time. When he'd succeeded in staying away by the simple action of putting an ocean between them.

He'd been supposed to study at the London School of Economics. At the last minute his father had talked to his mother, who'd pulled some strings and got him the chance of a place in Harvard. He'd known it was the right thing to do but it had broken something inside him.

Christ, he was a mess. He hadn't realized quite how much until she had walked back into his life. Maybe he was an idiot to go along with this. Maybe he should just walk away before he got in too deep. Because he suspected that he might never get enough of her.

He studied the purity of her features, her beauty only enhanced by the scar. Her face was a perfect oval, with high cheekbones, a narrow straight nose, and full, sculpted lips. He was almost overcome by an urge to lower his head and take those lips with his own. Slide his hands around that perfect ass and lift her onto the counter. The blood pooled in his groin, and his balls ached.

He stepped back. Just to prove he still could.

"Okay, so we do this then?" he asked.

"I told you, I'll talk to Jake and I'll get back to you. In the meantime, stick to the schedule you gave us. If you need to change anything let us know…and play nice with your babysitters. They're here for your protection."

"You're leaving?" He didn't want her to go. Not yet.

"I'm heading back to the office."

He wasn't going to let her go without a kiss, but as he leaned in, she slipped out from in front of him.

"I'll call you tonight," he said as she reached the door.

"I won't be there." And she was gone.

Chapter Eight

She'd stayed away for two whole days. Just to prove to herself that she could. But there was no avoiding Declan tonight. It was the first of his "business dinners" and her first go at being his "non-confrontational girlfriend."

She'd arranged to meet him here, wanting to make an entrance. To help with that, she'd borrowed a dress from Kim. She did own a long black dress that she used when she was on duty at parties and the like, but that dress, while elegant, was intended to make her merge into the background as much as possible. Tonight she needed to make a statement. She wanted people to notice her, so when she turned up on other occasions, she would already be imprinted on people's minds as Declan's girlfriend.

The dress was red. Apparently, Jake had a thing about red. Strapless, it left her shoulders bare, hugged her breasts, waist, and hips and then flared out in a fishtail. On her feet, she wore four-inch scarlet stilettoes—again borrowed from

Kim—she didn't want to think about what Kim had gotten up to in those shoes. But in them, Jess would tower over most of the other women there. She would be hard to forget.

She was also wearing makeup for the first time in…she couldn't actually remember how long. While she didn't dislike makeup, most of the time she just didn't see the point. But tonight, she wanted to look like something she wasn't, and the makeup was a mask. She'd used a cover stick to hide the scar, then foundation. It was weird seeing her face perfect. She missed the scar. It was part of her now. She'd smudged black under her lower lids, blue on her upper, lots of mascara to darken her lashes, and bright red lipstick that the packet promised was kiss-proof and would last twenty-four hours.

After handing her coat to the girl behind the counter, she headed into the main room and loitered just inside the door. She spotted Declan straightaway and her breath hitched in her throat. He stood across the room, talking with another man. Even with his back to her, he was stunning in a black tux that fitted his broad shoulders.

As if drawn by her stare, he turned slowly. His eyes widened when he saw her, and a slow smile curled his lips. He left the man he'd been speaking to without another word, strolled over, and came to a halt in front of her. His gaze wandered over her, leaving a trail of heat.

"You look…hot, sexy…stunning." He took a step closer, then his hand reached out to stroke down the line of her cheek. "You also look different without this."

"Like the old Jess?" Did she want him to say yes?

He shook his head slowly, still studying her. "No, not like the old Jess. She was a young girl. You're all woman." His hand dropped to his side. "Have you been avoiding me?"

"Yes."

A smile flickered across his face. "Scared?"

That was spot-on. But she bit back her inclination to snap something sarcastic and just bestowed him a gracious smile. "Not at all. We were just getting everything organized, going through the intel, and setting things up."

His eyes narrowed. Then he shrugged and glanced around the room. "Is there anything I should be doing?"

"Having fun? Mingling with the rich and influential?"

"I mean different than normal."

"No, just act as you normally do. There are a couple of high-level politicians here this evening, so security is huge. No one is going to try anything. Tonight is really in the way of a trial run, sort of see how you behave." In her new nice persona she gave a bright smile. "But I'm sure you'll do great."

Declan's brows drew together. "Are you being nice again?"

So much for being subtle. "Yes. But for real. I've decided it's time to put the past behind us. After all, ten years ago, you were young, immature, an asshole, a…"

He grinned. "You were doing so well…for about two seconds."

She took a deep breath and refixed her smile. "What I meant to say was we were both young and I can't blame you forever for breaking my immature heart. So, just to let you know, no hard feelings."

His eyelids drooped, and he watched her out of half-closed eyes. "Hmm. I'm thinking there's going to be lots of… hard feelings."

Why did her gaze drop straight to his groin?

• • •

Declan shoved his hands in his pockets, mainly to hide the fact that his dick was hard. Had been since she'd walked into the room in that red dress and once again rocked his world. He'd come alive as though a light switched on in his mind.

His gaze wandered down to where her scarlet-tipped toes peeped out from under the dress. In her four-inch heels, she was only a couple of inches shorter than he was. And she was quite the most beautiful thing he had ever seen.

He wanted to strip her out of that dress, though maybe she could keep the heels, and fuck her until he stopped thinking about the past. He didn't want her to be "nice." He wanted bad, filthy-dirty, no-holds-barred sex with her.

"Come on," she said, "time to mingle."

Looked like the sex was going to have to wait. It was going to be a long hard night.

The dinner was arranged by an organization McCabe Industries donated a lot of money to, a high-profile charity that he actually believed in. But he hated these events. He cast a sideways glance at Jess. At least he had no worry about being bored with Jess in tow. He could just imagine her without the dress, those long legs wrapped around him…

"Get your mind out of the gutter, Declan."

He grinned. "Just getting into the part. You are supposed to be my girlfriend after all."

The dinner was as bad as expected. Over the last few years, he'd felt increasingly alienated at these affairs. Like he was somehow in the wrong body and wanted to tear at his skin, get beneath it, find someone he could feel comfortable with, not continually irritated, rubbed up the wrong way, or even worse, bored out of his mind. But with Jess at his side, he could take it.

She stuck close beside him during the predinner mingling, playing the part of his girlfriend with a smooth ease. Her hand rested on his arm or his shoulder, and she didn't move away when he wrapped one arm around her waist to pull her close. Each touch stoked the heat inside him, but he welcomed the slow buildup because he was going to have her tonight. In every way he could think of. And then a few more.

At the dinner, he was seated opposite her. He hardly noticed the food, and as the speeches started, he sat back, kept his attention on Jess, and allowed his mind to wander.

He'd done everything his family had required of him; the company was now eminently respectable and worth about ten times more than when he'd taken control at twenty-five.

But he didn't give a crap. Some sort of premature midlife crisis? His dad obviously thought all he needed was the love of a good woman. Or even a bad one. His dad was crazy. Declan's gaze drifted across the table to where Jess was seated. She was leaning in close to the man on her right, smiling at something he said, and a flash of rage stabbed him in the gut.

Across the table she must have sensed his focus because she glanced up and met his stare. For long minutes he held her gaze. She licked her lips with a pointed pink tongue, leaving her full mouth glistening, moist scarlet, and heat pooled in his belly.

Without giving himself time to think, he pushed back his chair and got to his feet, ignoring the looks his neighbors cast his way.

He strode around the table to where she sat, her gaze never leaving him. Leaning down close, he whispered in her ear. "Time for us to show each other just how nice we can be."

She raised an eyebrow, but didn't move. "Aren't you supposed to be giving a speech later?"

"I don't care. Come on. I'm bored. Let's go have some fun." He rested his hands on her shoulders and blew gently in her ear, felt a shiver run through her. "We're making a scene here."

"You're making a scene," she murmured. "Most unlike you."

"And it's only going to get worse. My dick is so hard I thought it was going to spontaneously combust, probably taking the table with it.

Amusement flashed in her eyes, and then she swiped her tongue across her lower lip again and he groaned. But she gave a small nod and finally she pushed herself to her feet.

Before she could change her mind, he took her arm and hustled her toward the door. "This is good, though," he said. "Obviously I can't keep my hands off you so that helps the cover story."

He needed to kiss her, suck her plump lower lip into his mouth, push his tongue inside her. Unfortunately as they exited the room, they picked up his babysitters and he groaned in frustration.

The car was waiting out in front. Jess had a quiet word with the guards; one peeled away and the other opened the back door for them. Declan waited for Jess to get in, then climbed in beside her. The guard got in beside the driver, and they pulled away.

Declan leaned forward and pushed the button that brought the tinted glass divider up between the front and the rear seats, and then he sat back and hauled Jess into his arms.

One hand slid behind her neck to drag her close and pull her head down for his kiss. He didn't hold back, his lips hard against hers, parting them, pushing inside her hot, wet mouth. Deep, drugging kisses, that were nowhere near enough.

Finally he ran out of oxygen, released her, and sat back, his breath coming hard and fast. How long did they have? He suspected not long enough to get her out of that dress and onto his cock.

While he was considering options, she pulled away slightly. He looked at her, ready to drag her back into his arms, but something in her eyes stopped him.

"I still owe you," she said and the look in her eyes made the last of the blood drain to his pulsing erection.

He went still, every muscle locked tight. "So you do." His voice sounded hoarse to his ears as she slipped from his lap to kneel on the floor. He spread his thighs, and she shuffled closer until she knelt between his legs.

Her lips parted slightly, and her tongue poked out between her teeth. She rested her palm on his thigh and he jumped; then she stroked upward, and he lost the ability to move. Finally, her fingers closed around the length of his shaft and she squeezed.

A groan escaped him and his head fell back against the leather of the seat. He watched through his lashes as she flicked open the button on his pants and slowly lowered the zipper. The relief was amazing and lasted about two seconds.

She tugged at his pants and he lifted his hips allowing her to pull them down, then she settled back. "Is this *nice* enough for you, Declan?"

But he'd lost the ability to speak.

Reaching behind her, she loosened her hair, so it fell about her shoulders. Her perfume, sweet and sharp, swirled in the air, filling his nostrils. Then she leaned closer and breathed over the head of his cock. It jerked.

Christ, he was going to lose it if she didn't take him soon. No, she wasn't being nice. Not nice at all.

Finally, she licked him, a long slow stroke from the base to the head. Her tongue swirled around and heat flooded him. Then she took him in the hot, wet cavern of her mouth, and it was the most amazing thing he had ever experienced. His hips rose from the seat, pushing himself into her mouth, unable to control the movement.

She pulled away, sat back on her heels, and pouted.

It was official. She was so not nice.

When he thought he might beg, she wrapped her hand around the base of his shaft and squeezed, then lowered her lips to him once more, engulfing him in the moistness of her mouth.

She took him deep, alternating with hard sucks to the head while her fingers shifted lower and caressed his balls. He watched her every move, unable to drag his eyes from the most erotic thing he had ever seen. She'd always loved doing this to him. He'd forgotten. Or wiped it from his mind. But she'd gone down on him everywhere and anywhere. Giving him her total concentration as though his cock was the most important thing in her world.

Sweat beaded on his forehead as the pleasure built inside him, tugging at his balls, tightening his spine. Until he could hold it back no longer. His back arched and he exploded into her mouth. She kept sucking and swallowing and pleasure washed over him in waves, until finally he was done. Wrapping his hands in her silky hair, he slowed her movement, finally holding her still.

She pulled away and peered up at him, lush red lips curved into a smile. "I told you I was nice."

Chapter Nine

As she sat back on her heels, Jess became aware of the movement of the vehicle. They must have halted at traffic lights, because now they were pulling away and picking up speed.

Declan sprawled in front of her, his clothes still in disarray, making no attempt to cover himself. "Baby, 'nice' doesn't come into it."

She licked her lips and he groaned. Again. She could still taste the saltiness of him; she'd forgotten how much she loved to take him like that. The sensation of all that masculine power under her command. Declan, usually so in control, losing it totally, coming apart for her.

A pulse beat insistently between her thighs, but she refused to give in to it. Anyway, there was no way sex in this dress in a moving car was possible, and she wasn't getting naked with two of her men up front, even if they couldn't see through the tinted glass. Knowing her luck, they'd get pulled over or a puncture or…

She rested her hands on his knees and pushed herself up and into the seat beside him, then hooked her long hair behind her ears. "Well, that was more fun than a stuffy charity dinner."

Declan shifted on the seat pulling up his pants. She sighed. She liked disheveled Declan much better than Billionaire-Perfect-CEO Declan. But it was just as well, maybe she needed the reminder that he was really no different from the other guys she'd been trying to date.

As he finished zipping up his pants, he turned to her, his gaze dropping down over her body, then past her and out of the window. They were driving along the embankment now and she could make out the dark slow moving water of the river.

"You want to go for a walk?" he asked.

Suddenly she had the urge to be outside, in the fresh air and she nodded. "Why not?"

Declan pressed the intercom button and spoke quietly and a few seconds later, the car pulled up to the side of the road and came to a halt. The guard got out from the front and opened the door and she climbed out. Declan followed her and they stood for a moment. He stripped off his jacket and rested it over her bare shoulders. She hadn't even noticed the chill air.

Peering around her into the night, she saw nothing suspicious. But she had no real worry about his safety tonight. There was no way they'd been followed; the streets were too quiet.

The city was never dark, and the streetlights reflected on the water. Declan took her arm, and they walked along beside the river, breathing in the dank, salty air. She was aware of the guard falling into step about thirty feet behind them, but she ignored his presence. She cast a sideways glance at Declan. Once again, he looked perfect, hard to believe five minutes earlier, he'd had his pants around his knees and she'd had his dick in her mouth. Now, he looked what he was: a super-successful businessman. She probably looked like a hooker he'd picked up.

Something occurred to her that was quite mind-blowing. She came to a halt as she thought it through. "You know, Rory was right."

Declan stopped beside her and in the light from a nearby streetlamp she could see his frown. "He was?"

"Much as I hate to admit it, because I don't like him very much, but yeah. I'd never fit into your world."

His frown deepened, forming lines between his dark brows. "You could. You could do anything if you wanted it enough" He reached out and tucked a stray strand of hair behind her ear, and she shivered at the caress. "You certainly look the part."

She shrugged. "I borrowed the dress. And the shoes. But really, I have no interest in dressing up. And parties and posh dinners leave me cold. If I'd managed to keep hold of you all those years ago, I'd have been bored out of my mind. No doubt I'd have done something really stupid just to liven things up, and your Mr. Perfect facade would have flown out the window."

"I'm not perfect."

"Hah. Come on, Declan, I've read up on you. You never put a foot out of place; there's not a hint of scandal or gossip attached to you."

"You make me sound…boring."

She grinned. "If the cap fits…."

He took a step closer so his chest brushed against her breasts, and a tingle ran through her. Then a shiver, and she hugged his jacket around her. The night was cool, that was all. He lowered his head and his warm breath feathered across her ear. "Do you think I'm boring, Jess?"

He didn't give her chance to answer; his hands rested on her shoulders and he gently urged her backward, until she came up against the barrier to the river. They were in the shadow of a huge pillar, and she didn't protest as he lowered his head and kissed her.

The kiss lasted only seconds but left her shaken. She cleared her throat. "I thought we were walking."

A slow smile curved his lips, but to her shock, he slipped his hand in hers and tugged her out. She hadn't held hands since…since the last time she had walked like this with Declan all those years ago. They hadn't been able to be together without touching.

His palm was hot in hers, but his grip was loose. She could pull free if she wanted to, but she didn't. They walked slowly; she couldn't do much else in her four-inch heels.

"Why did you join the army?" he asked, breaking the silence.

"Maybe I had an overwhelming urge to go and shoot things, and it seemed sensible to do it in a controlled environment."

"Really?"

She thought for a moment. To be honest, that time in her life was a bit of a haze. She hadn't been thinking of much at all, keeping her mind blank so as not to remember things she'd rather forget.

"I didn't know what I wanted to do except I couldn't face

going back to school. Then I saw a recruitment ad for the army and thought why not? It seemed as good as anything."

"And did you like it?"

"Some bits. I liked blowing things up. I liked the physical side of things, and I loved training. I even enjoyed the danger in a weird sort of way."

"You never feel so alive as when there's a chance you might die?"

She flashed a glance at his face, then down to his arm. "I suppose you'd know how that feels now. Anyway, the discipline was good for me, however much I hated it."

"So why did you leave?"

"I never really got used to taking orders, especially from total assholes. I made sergeant twice and got busted down again. Then Jake—he was an officer in my unit—left and started up Knight Security. He offered me a job, and I took it. End of story."

"You sleeping with him?"

"With Jake?" She snorted. "You have got to be kidding."

"Why not?"

Basically, because even if he'd been interested, and maybe back before he'd met Kim, he might have been, she had given up on men. And she hadn't wanted to lose Jake as a friend. He was one of the few guys she respected. Also, she'd tried sleeping around and always ended up comparing them to what she'd had with Declan and been devastatingly disappointed. But she didn't want to share that little piece of information. "Jake's married to my best friend," she said instead. "He's been in love with her forever. But he's been a good friend and a good boss."

"So are you seeing anyone now?"

"That's none of your business."

"Baby, you just gave me a blowjob, I think that makes it my business. But I'm guessing there's no one and hasn't been for a while."

Now she did try and tug her hand free, but his grip tightened. "And why would you think that."

"Because you felt like a virgin."

"Have you had lots of virgins, Declan?"

He cast her a sideways glance. "Only one. But I remember it well."

She swallowed. So did she; the night they first made love was indelibly imprinted in her dreams. He'd made her come with his mouth until she was so wet that he had pushed in with ease, only causing her the slightest hitch of pain.

"But it wasn't only that. You were desperate that day in my office. I'm guessing there hasn't been anyone for a while."

She wanted to argue that she hadn't been desperate, but it would be a lie and she wanted to keep lies to a minimum. "Maybe. I told you, I've been quite happy with my vibrator, so what the hell would I need a man for?"

"I thought you were looking for a 'nice' man."

"That's only recent. I joined a dating agency." Though she was still waiting for her first offering since Kim had doctored her questionnaire. It made her wonder what her friend had put down.

Declan turned to face her, brows drawn together. "I'm not sure I like the idea of you dating other men."

She had a fuzzy, warm feeling at that, which terrified the life out of her. Christ, she wasn't even dating Declan. "Well, get over it. Because it really isn't any of your business."

Without waiting for him to answer, she headed back.

They didn't speak again. When they reached the car, she spoke to the driver. "Drop me off at the office, on the way." She'd get a cab from there. Suddenly she was filled with the need to be alone. She wanted to be away from Declan because his words had confused her. It was nothing to do with him who she dated. This was about sex. Nothing else. She wouldn't allow it to be about anything else.

They sat in silence as far apart as they could get, but strangely it was a peaceful silence. He didn't speak until she was climbing out of the car. "Thanks for the blowjob. Maybe next time I'll return the favor."

"I'll look forward to it." Next time wouldn't be for an age; she had plans for the rest of the weekend, though she was doing her best not to think about those plans too closely. But then something occurred to her and she leaned back into the car. "Are you serious about wanting some...fun?"

He quirked a brow. "What do you have in mind?"

"Meet me at the O2 Arena tomorrow morning at ten. And dress casual."

"Why? What—"

But she straightened, slammed the door, and walked away.

• • •

The car pulled up just inside the gates, and Declan sat for a moment staring out of the window and trying to decide what Jess was up to. What she had planned. From the amusement in Steve's eyes, Declan was pretty sure his bodyguard knew what was going down, but if so, he wasn't sharing.

Declan had done a lot of thinking last night after she'd

left him. In many ways she was right; they were totally unsuitable. Back then, they would never have made it long-
term. They'd both been young, impressionable; the affair
had been cut short and so attained far more importance
than it ever should have. Now, he suspected he was drawn to
her because of the whole unfinished-business thing.

He'd never admit it, but those first months after he'd
left her had been hell. He'd asked his father to keep an eye
on her, to tell him if she needed anything, to pass on his
number if she got in touch—he'd never meant to cut her
off completely. He'd thought perhaps they could have been
friends. Friends with an ocean between them to keep him
from temptation.

And every single day he'd waited for a call.

A call that never came.

So he'd done what he always did and ignored his feelings,
locked them up inside and immersed himself in what he had
to do.

Of course, now he knew that she'd gone to see his father.
Something his dad had failed to mention and one day soon
they'd have a discussion about that. But maybe his dad had
done the right thing, because if Jess had called, he would
have gone running. And as she'd pointed out, they'd have
been a disaster together.

So keep that in mind. This was about closure. And sex.
Christ, he wanted her again. He wondered whether her idea
of fun this morning would involve them getting hot, naked,
and sweaty together. He hoped so, but considering the location, somehow he doubted it.

He climbed out of the car and glanced around. In front
of him was the huge white dome of the arena. In front of that,

a small crowd milled around what looked to be some sort of bright orange crane device that reached high in the sky. He searched for Jess in the crowd, but couldn't see her until a movement to the side drew his attention. She was walking across the space between the building and the crane, wearing black jeans and a matching long-sleeved T-shirt. She caught his gaze; her face was pale and her lips held in a tight line.

He strode across, came to a halt in front of her. "Are you okay?"

"Do I look okay?" She scowled. "Actually, I've just puked up my breakfast."

"Rough night?"

"No. Rough morning. Or it's soon going to be." She glanced at the crane behind him and swallowed. "Why the hell did I agree to this?"

He turned slightly and followed her gaze. "Just exactly what is 'this'?"

"You haven't guessed? Well, I hope you like heights because we're going bungee jumping. Off that." She nodded toward the crane. It looked pretty high. "One hundred and sixty meters," she said.

"Are you kidding me?" But his gut tightened at the thought. And not in a bad way.

"Wish I was. It's for one of Dani's doggy charities. I agreed to do it in a drunken moment."

"And where do I come in?"

"I just checked, and they'll let us jump together. They even have a name for it, a tandem jump." She looked him up and down. "And is that your idea of casual?"

He glanced at his black pants and black sweater. "Yeah."

She snorted. But he ignored the sound. A grin tugged at

his face. He'd never done a bungee jump before. He looked from the crane back to Jess. "Fantastic."

"Fantastic? You have to be kidding." She shook her head. "We're going first because otherwise I'm going to lose my nerve as well as my breakfast. Come on. We need to get weighed."

She stalked off toward the small crowd and he followed. There were a group of guys wearing black sweatshirts with "Bungee Team" across the back. Jess halted in front of them. "Let's get this done."

One man led them to a weighing machine. He weighed Jess twice, wrote a number on the back of her hand, and called the weight out to his friend. He repeated the procedure with Declan and then waved them to the cage at the bottom of the crane.

Declan studied Jess's face as a second man ran through the safety procedures while he fastened a harness around their waists and ankles. Jess checked each of the fastenings, tugging at the leather.

"Are you sure it's tight enough?"

The man grinned. "I'm sure. We've never lost one yet."

"There's a first time for everything," she muttered.

"Okay, into the cage," he said, gesturing to the orange cage. Jess bit her lip and then shuffled over, Declan followed.

"Right, for the jump you're going to be close together. As close as you can get. Jess, wrap your arms around Declan's waist and tuck your head right in against his neck. Declan you hold her around the shoulders."

Declan wrapped his arms around her and pulled her close, felt her arms come around his middle and hold him tight, so she was plastered against the length of his body. She burrowed her face in the curve of his shoulder. A tremble ran through her.

He hadn't thought she was scared of anything. He couldn't decide whether to laugh or to throw her over his shoulder and carry her to safety. Then the gate was closing, shutting them in, the cage jerked beneath them, and they were rising into the air.

"Oh God."

He rubbed a hand down her back, then looked around him. One of the bungee team guys was in the cage with them, but Declan zoned him out as they rose. The view was amazing. Three-hundred-and-sixty degrees over the city. For once the sky was blue, the sunlight sparkling on the dark water of the river now far below them. Jess's head was once again shoved in his shoulder.

"Come on, Jess, take a look. You're missing all the fun."

"Fuck off," she mumbled.

He chuckled, and she lifted her head and glared. At least her eyes were open, though they fixed on him not the view. Maybe time to try and distract her. He pressed his hips against hers, letting her know his cock liked having her wrapped around him so close.

Her eyes widened. "I can't believe you can do *that* at a moment like *this*."

He chuckled again, but his dick was becoming painful and he shifted a little away from her.

"So have you done this before?" he asked.

"Are you crazy? Do you think I'd be here now if I had?"

"But you knew you were scared of heights?"

A visible shudder ran through her. "Yes. I've jumped out of planes during training."

"And you were okay?"

"Of course I wasn't okay. What sort of normal person jumps out of planes? I puked before and after."

"So why are you doing this if you're afraid of heights?"

"I told you, it's for charity. Plus, I was somewhat under the influence when I agreed. But…"

"But…?" he urged.

"I think you need to face your fears head-on. It's the only way to defeat them. But I swear if the rope breaks, I will never forgive Dani."

He peered over the edge. "No, probably not."

She followed his gaze and went a little greener. "Holy shit."

He smiled. "I'll hold on to you."

"You might change your mind if I throw up on you on the way down."

"You won't. You're the bravest person I know."

The cage jolted to a halt, and she gave a little squeak. She really was scared and he was filled with an overwhelming urge to protect her from her fears. Make them go away. "We don't have to do this, Jess. We can just ride back down. I'll match whatever you're raising from the jump. Your friend's doggies won't lose out."

Her spine stiffened, her jaw clenched. "No way."

The gate opened, and they were teetering on the edge. The ground looked a long, long way away. He felt a flash of fear and grinned. At least he wasn't bored. Maybe Jess didn't fit into his world, but she certainly made it a brighter place.

"Oh. My. God."

She clung to him like her life depended on it. He liked the feeling.

"You want a push?" the bungee guy asked. "Or are you going to jump?"

"We'll jump," he said.

Pulling her even closer, he stared out at the view, the world laid out before him, Jess in his arms. His gut churned; his adrenaline spiked. "You ready?" He felt the slightest nod against him.

Taking a last deep breath, he leaped out into open space. Then he was diving head first toward the Earth. Jess's arms tightened around him, her fingers digging into the skin at his waist, her scream muffled in the curve where his neck met his shoulder. And in that moment, free-falling through the sky, the hard ground racing toward him, he knew he didn't want to ever let her go.

He had a split second to brace himself for the jolt, but it never came. The deceleration was smooth, and then they were rising again.

Bouncing on the end of a rope, his woman in his arms, it occurred it him that life with Jess would never be boring.

She thought they were getting each other out of their systems. She was wrong. He just had to work out the right time and place to explain that to her.

Finally, they stopped moving, someone grabbed his shoulders and lowered him to the ground. Jess wriggled free. Her face was white, and he leaned toward her and pressed a kiss to her forehead. "That was fun. You want to go again?"

She curled her lip in a snarl. "Bugger off."

Chapter Ten

Declan had changed after the jump. There had been something in his eyes she couldn't recognize, but it had made her twitch. Determination? But what was he determined to do?

Anyway, it made her nervous, but not enough to stop seeing him. Rather it had made her more desperate to get as much as she possibly could of him before everything went to shit.

It was five days since the jump, and they'd had sex every one of those days. Lots of sex. Quick sex, slow sex, at his office, in his apartment. She couldn't keep her hands off him. Though she refused to spend the night, which he said was a pain because he wanted early morning sex with her all sleepy and tousled.

But that was getting into dangerous territory.

She needed to get a little distance, but more than that, she needed to prove to herself that she could control this thing between them. Because there was something between them. Even if it was only sex, it was there. Drawing them together.

All the time in his presence she sensed him watching her, wanting her. It made her body twitch with need, until her dreams were filled with Declan and each morning she awoke, hot, bothered, restless, and ready for more sex.

Now, watching him across the room, cool, remote, businesslike, she decided she was worrying too much. In just over a week, the court case would start. After that, presumably Declan would no longer need protection. And there would be no reason for them to ever see each other again.

She hated the shaft of pain that pierced her at the thought.

Looking away, her gaze clashed with Jake, who watched her, his brows drawn together as though he were picking away at a particularly interesting puzzle.

They were in a meeting, this time in Jake's office. Jake had wanted to meet their newest client. No doubt he'd been listening to office gossip.

The two men had sized each other up, then shook hands, one of those testosterone-fueled handshakes that always looked like they'd result in broken fingers. But she got the feeling that Jake respected Declan, and it took a lot to impress her boss.

Dave and Steve were also present. The guys were all seated, but Jess was too restless and she paced the room, listening while Jake outlined a plan for drawing out Declan's attackers. For the first time, it occurred to her that there was actually danger involved. That there was a small chance they would get to Declan, maybe hurt him, even kill him. These guys were serious. Something unexpected and almost unidentifiable twisted inside her.

She was afraid. Not the adrenaline-inducing fear of the bungee jump, but something much darker. Plonking herself down on the edge of the sofa, she tried to get a grip on her fear.

"You okay, Jess?" Jake asked.

She rubbed the spot above the bridge of her nose as she thought about her answer. She suspected the correct response was "no." She was pretty sure she was not okay. Instead, she tried to give a casual shrug. "Just having second thoughts. I'm not sure we should be playing around with these guys."

"And have you an alternate suggestion?" Jake asked.

"Up the security. Keep him safe until after the court case."

Jake turned to Declan. "How do you feel about all this? Are you okay to go ahead?"

Something flashed across his face and then was gone. He shrugged. "Whatever you think best."

Did he want this over with? Including her? A week ago, she would have said yes. Now she wasn't so sure. "We go ahead then."

Declan rose to his feet. "Will you walk me out?" he said to her.

She followed him out of the room, eyes glued to his very impressive ass. At the elevator she pressed the button for the ground floor and gestured for him to enter.

"You don't need to worry about me," he said as the doors closed behind them.

She shrugged again. "It won't do the firm's reputation any good if we lose a client. Especially now, when Jake's stepping down. So I'd prefer it if you didn't get yourself killed."

He leaned back against the wall of the elevator. "Maybe I should get a gun."

"I don't think so." She shuddered. Clients with guns were not on top of her things-I-want list. "Can you shoot?"

"Never tried. Never even held a gun."

"Never? Really?" She considered him for a moment. "You want to?" Was she just looking for an excuse to keep him here? Probably. But what the hell. "Or have you got an important meeting to go to? You look like you have an important meeting." He was dressed in a sharp charcoal-gray suit, crisp white shirt, and dark red tie and looked the perfect executive. Except for maybe the restlessness in his silver-gray eyes. It occurred to her that maybe he wasn't happy with his perfect life.

When they'd been teenagers, she'd always known that under the controlled exterior had lurked a wild boy. It was what had drawn her to him. What had pushed her to get a reaction from him. She'd believed when they met again, that the wild boy was entirely eradicated beneath the perfect veneer of sophistication. But he wasn't gone entirely. He might show a perfect front to the world, but beneath the glossy facade there was a volcano waiting to explode. There always had been. Her question was did Declan have more or less control now than he'd had ten years ago?

But why should she care.

He studied her for a moment. Then pulled his cell phone out of his pocket and pressed speed dial. "Paul? Cancel my meetings this morning. Something's come up." He closed the call before the other man could speak and turned back to her.

Heat coiled in her belly, and her heart rate picked up. Leaning across him, she pressed the button for the basement.

It was quiet down on the lower level. There were a lot of cases at the moment and most of the operatives were out on assignment. At the far end of the corridor, she punched in the code for the shooting range, then pressed her thumb to the pad. The door clicked open. Jake had contacts that facilitated them getting the licenses for their firearms, but there were strict rules for their storage.

The room was big, but narrow, and the longer side ran along the whole depth of the building. It consisted of a counter that spanned this end of the room, and then the room was split into three alleys. She paused just inside the door, glanced at him, then turned back and locked it behind them. Declan's eyebrows rose, but he didn't say anything as she led him to the gun safe at the far corner of the room, and again input the code and pressed her thumb to the pad. Declan shrugged out of his jacket and tossed it on the counter and rolled up his sleeves.

She selected a Sig Pro 9mm—one of her favorites—and a magazine. She turned and handed it to Declan, minus the bullets.

"It's not very big," he murmured. The weapon did look small in his large hand.

"It's big enough." She took the gun from him. "You need to insert the magazine, like so. Then to load the chamber you pull back the slide, like this"—she demonstrated—"and release it. Easy. Here you go."

After removing the magazine and bullet, she handed the gun and ammunition to Declan. He slotted the magazine, chambered the bullet. "Now what?"

"Take out the bullets. We'll have a go without them first."

She stood behind him, stepping up close so she could feel the heat of his skin though his clothes. "Now," she said, "grip your pistol firm in both hands, but keep your finger off the trigger until you're ready to shoot." Her hands rested on his upper arms, steadying him, and a prickle of awareness ran through her.

"Your feet should be shoulder-width apart." Jess slipped a leg between his and nudged them apart. "Stretch out your arms, and lean slightly forward, but stay balanced. Now take a deep breath, exhale halfway, hold it, and squeeze the trigger."

He squeezed, the pistol made a slight clicking noise.

"Okay, let's try it with bullets. Load up."

Declan took the magazine from her and reloaded competently while she pressed a button. Halfway down the room, a target swung into position. Jess stepped to the side this time, leaving him alone, and he took up the stance she had shown him, arms outstretched, feet apart. He closed one eye, sighted down the line of the pistol, took a deep breath, and squeezed.

He was good. A natural. Most people jumped a mile when they first felt the recoil, but he stood easy and relaxed. He hadn't hit the center of the target though, which made her feel slightly better and brought a frown to his face. She was guessing Declan liked to do everything perfectly

"Again," she said. He was slightly better this time but still failed to hit the center.

Jess took the gun from his hand, spun round, and shot a bullet into the center of the target without even aiming.

"Show-off," he muttered.

She gave him back the gun. "Once more." She moved back behind him, rested her hands lightly on his hips, turning him slightly. "Focus on the target. Clear your mind of everything else."

"That's a little hard with your hands all over me." But this time he hit the target right in the center.

She still had her hands on his hips and she squeezed. "Put the gun down, Declan."

A subtle tension ran through his body, but he removed the magazine from the pistol and rested them gently on the counter. He didn't turn, just stood, hands loose at his side. Jess stepped up closer until she was pressed against the length of his back. She slid her hands around from where they rested on his hips to his groin.

"Jesus."

"Just checking if anything else has come up," she murmured. He was becoming hard beneath her palm and heat sank through her body, pooling in her belly, then lower, so her sex tingled and an insistent pulse set up between her thighs.

She needed this.

She tugged his shirt out of his pants, then flicked open the button and lowered the zipper. Pushing her hands inside, she found him hot and hard. She wrapped her fingers around the steely length and squeezed.

He did move then. Grasping her wrist, he tugged her hand out from inside his pants, then turned around, lowered his head, and kissed her. Deep, wet kisses that filled her mouth and made her breasts ache.

With his hands gripping her hips, he picked her up and placed her on the counter without ever breaking the kiss. She was gasping for air now, need filling her as he nudged open her thighs. She tore open his shirt, buttons flying across the room, but she had to touch him. His skin was burning hot. She hardly noticed as he dragged her jacket from her shoulders, threw it to the floor. Her shirt followed, then her bra. At last he released her mouth and she took in huge breaths of air, filling her starving lungs.

Lowering his head, he sucked one tight nipple into his mouth, then bit down, and she gasped. He repeated the process with the other, alternating stinging bites with soothing strokes of his tongue until she was mindless with need.

His hands were at her waist now, unfastening her pants, and she arched her hips up off the counter to allow him to drag them down over her long legs, tugging off her shoes without slowing until she was entirely naked, sprawled on the counter before him. Now his movements slowed. He straightened, gazing down at her with eyes darkened and a dull flush across his cheekbones.

"Lie back." When she didn't move fast enough, he placed a hand on her shoulder and pushed her gently until her spine rested against the smooth, cool metal of the counter. He trailed his hand down over her breast, rubbing the engorged nipple so sensations shot to her groin. Then lower so it splayed across her flat belly.

"Tell me," he said. "Did you bring me down here just to seduce me?"

She didn't hesitate. "Yes."

He chuckled, but then the laugh stilled in his throat. He dug his fingers into the soft skin of her stomach, then dragged them lower through the pale blond curls. She came up on her elbows because she didn't want to miss any of this, holding her breath, waiting for the first touch.

His gaze was fixed on her sex as he slowly slid a finger along the seam and her thighs widened of their own accord, her hips rising to push against his hand. His finger slipped inside.

"Jesus, you are so wet."

He parted her with one hand, then trailed his fingers over the drenched folds, stopping just short of her swollen clit, so she bucked her hips in protest. Then back down to push inside her, first one finger, then a second, rubbing at her inner walls so her flesh tingled and tightened around him.

Then finally, he lowered his head and kissed her. He used his mouth and his tongue, long strokes along the length of her sex, pushing inside, nibbling at the outer lips, sucking and licking. Heat washed through her in waves, threatening to drag her under.

She growled low in her throat as he circled her clit, never quite touching, until she thought she might go mad with need. His hands were splayed on her inner thighs now, holding her open to him, holding her still, while he continued his slow torture.

"Please, Declan."

He glanced up and his darkened eyes captured hers. "I like it when you beg. Say it again."

"Please."

She could feel his warm breath blowing over her, and her muscles clenched. "You want this?" He dropped the lightest of kisses on the tight little nub and the breath left her in a *whoosh*. She held herself perfectly still, waiting for his next touch, then nearly jumped as the tip of his tongue teased her until she thought she would go mad with the need for release. He lapped at her gently, and she could feel her orgasm building, tightening everything inside her.

Finally, his mouth closed over her and he suckled her clit into his mouth, and she shattered into a million pieces. Her eyes clamped closed as the pleasure washed over her in waves, her hips pushing against him. As the pleasure ebbed, he bit down and she came again. He straightened, but she was hardly aware as he put on a condom and positioned himself between her thighs.

She opened her eyes as he pushed inside, her inner muscles spasming around him as he filled her in one hard push of his hips. He ground against her sensitive clit, and she gasped his name.

There had never been anything like this. No one had ever come close to making her feel this way. Only Declan. That's why she had given up searching in the end.

At the thought, she had a flash of fear.

But it was only sex.

Mind-blowing, earth-shattering sex. He was pumping into her now, long, hard strokes, and she closed her eyes and let the feelings expand, spiral out of control until she lost all awareness except for the huge shaft between her legs, the hot mouth at her breast.

He sped up and she knew he was close, could feel the tenseness of his muscles, the sheer force of his concentration. He slipped a hand between them, massaged her clit, and she tipped over the edge once more as he spilled inside her.

For long minutes neither of them moved. Jess became aware of the hard metal at her back, the edge of the counter digging into her thighs. The air smelled of sex and sweat and Declan, and she breathed in deeply. Someone rattled at the door, but went away when they got no response.

Finally, she managed to move a hand and make a feeble attempt to push him off. Her legs were wrapped around his waist, and she unlocked them. He put a palm flat on the counter beside her and pushed himself up.

"Fuck," he said and ran his other hand through his hair. At least he'd lost his perfect businessman look. She pushed herself up on her elbows for a better view as he pulled out of her and stepped back.

A shiver ran through her, a feeling of emptiness that only Declan could fill. It was a feeling she remembered so well from the days after he left her. Another shiver ran through her. Fear, this time. She would not go through that again. But already she wanted to be back in his arms, and that terrified her.

His eyes held a sleepy satiated expression and a slow smile curved his lips. "That was…"

"Just sex," she said and jumped off the counter. After searching the floor for her clothes, she picked up her panties and clutched them in her hand.

His smile faded, and his brows drew together. He straightened his clothes, fastening his jacket over his ripped shirt and was once again the perfect businessman. "You know, it doesn't have to be 'just sex.'"

She glanced at him, a frown forming between her brows. "Oh yes, it does."

"Why? We're good together. There's no reason we shouldn't keep on being good together."

Was he crazy? "Are you crazy?"

"It makes perfect sense to me."

"Hah. Been there. Done that. Never happening again."

"It wouldn't be the same. We're different people than we

were ten years ago."

"Really, because you seem pretty much the same to me, Mr. Perfect." She yanked her panties up her legs, grabbed her pants and shirt, pulled them on. "And how long will it take before you realize...*again*...that I don't fit into your perfect world."

"Is that really how you see me?"

"Oh yeah. And I think I get it. That's how you were brought up to be. Your parents blackmailed you into thinking you always had to do the right thing. Suddenly I'm acceptable, and you think you want me. " She bent down and pulled her shoes on, then grabbed the pistol and took it back to the gun safe, locking it, before turning back to Declan. "But by now, you're so used to doing what's right, that you have no clue what you really want."

"I want you." He took a step toward her and she backed away.

"You just think you want me. Well, perhaps it's time you realized you don't always get what you want, Declan." Grabbing her jacket she stalked to the door, unlocked it, and turned back. "See yourself out."

She needed some time alone. He'd knocked her off balance with his crazy suggestions. Unfortunately, when she entered her office five minutes later, Jake was seated at her desk. She so didn't need this right now. Stifling a groan, she plastered a smile on her face.

"Anything I can help you with, boss?"

"I just got a report there was a problem with the shooting range. Someone had apparently barricaded themselves in."

"Hardly barricaded." She shrugged and plonked herself in the chair opposite. "Declan wanted to shoot a gun. As part of my new be-nice-to-clients image I thought, why not?"

"And…?"

"And…" She thought quickly. "And he'd never held a gun before so I thought he might be a little trigger happy. So in the interests of safety I locked the door."

He regarded her for a few seconds. "Nice try, but I'm not buying it."

What a surprise. "You're not? Any particular bit of it?"

"All of it."

There wasn't a lot she could say to that, so she stretched out her legs and examined her fingernails.

"What's going on between you and McCabe? And don't tell me nothing. You couldn't take your eyes off him in that meeting, and then afterward you lock yourself in the shooting range with him. And now, you look decidedly flushed and your shirt is inside out."

She glanced down. So it was. No getting anything past Jake. "We're having a thing."

"A thing?"

"You know a…thing. But you don't have to worry. It's not interfering with the job. I have everything organized."

"Maybe I'm not worried about the job. Maybe I'm worried about you."

"Sweet." Actually it was. "But as I said, I have everything under control."

"Why do I doubt that? Probably because you've never shown any interest in a client before. Hell, in anyone before. Have you any idea what you're doing?"

"Of course I do." Actually, she had no clue. But she was working it out slowly. Declan was obviously going through some sort of weird midlife crisis—being shot and almost blown up would do that to you—and had decided that she was the answer. He was totally deluded. "Actually, I'm doing what you told me to do and putting the past behind me."

His eyes narrowed. "Declan McCabe is your past?"

"My very, very distant past."

No way was she going to act as some sort of antidote just because Declan's perfect life suddenly didn't seem so perfect. Because he'd finally get over his little crisis and then he'd no doubt dump her like he had last time. Well, she wasn't going to give him the opportunity. From now on, she was keeping her distance.

She'd thought that she could have him, at least up until the trial, and then their lives would naturally go different ways. But if he was going to try and delude himself there could be more to this that just sex, then she had no choice.

He was an addiction and the only way to deal with addiction was a clean cut.

So no more sex with Declan.

• • •

Jess was wrong. He always got what he wanted.

But she wasn't wrong about everything. In fact she was spot-on with certain things. It was scary how clearly she saw him. It was true he'd never had to think about what he wanted before, because he'd always known exactly what he had to do. Except for that one glitch with Jess, he'd done everything his family had asked of him.

And look what that had gotten him.

He was bored. He admitted it—to himself at least. These days the job was all too easy. There was no challenge. And sometimes he felt as though he would explode if he had to sit through one more meeting.

But with Jess in his life, it didn't seem so bad. Except she was hardly in his life. He hadn't seen her over the weekend, and she hadn't answered his calls. She'd popped in briefly this morning to go over his schedule and then promptly vanished again. She was driving him to distraction.

She made him feel alive as he hadn't felt in years. Since he was eighteen in fact. And he wasn't ready to let that go yet. Was pretty sure he would never be ready. But she was fighting the obvious attraction.

He'd hurt her ten years ago when he'd walked away, but he hadn't realized how much. He'd believed her so young that she would get over it quickly. But she hadn't. A core of bitterness was wrapped around her heart, and she was running scared. He'd seen flashes of fear in her eyes when he'd suggested there might be more between them than sex.

She didn't trust him, and she didn't want more. Or at least that's what she was no doubt telling herself.

And could he blame her?

Maybe not, but he wasn't letting her go. She'd said it was good to face your fears. So it was time she faced this one.

He picked up his phone and pressed her number.

"What is it?" She sounded annoyed.

"I thought I might come over and we—"

"Sorry, no can do. I'm getting ready to go out."

He went still and his hand tightened on the phone. "Out where?"

"Not that it's any of your business, but I have a date. A date with a 'nice' man."

Keep cool. He was pretty sure this was just her running

scared. But scared or not, no way was she running into the arms of another man. "Anyone, I know?"

"I doubt it."

"Give me a name."

She was silent for a few seconds, then he could almost hear her mental shrug. "Harry Cantrell. He's a lawyer."

"Sounds boring. Stand him up, and I'll come over instead. You can introduce me to your vibrator. I've been having these amazing fantasies ever since we had phone sex." That was no lie; just the thought made his cock stand to attention.

"Never going to happen. But maybe Harry would like to meet my vibrator."

He gritted his teeth. "Don't even think about taking him back to your place."

"Or else what?" She didn't wait for an answer just disconnected.

He stared at his phone, while he thought about calling her back. But he had a suspicion she wouldn't pick up and that would piss him off even more. He needed a plan.

Actually though, he did know Harry Cantrell. He'd met him at one of his father's parties and Harry was not "nice." A criminal lawyer, he had a number of his dad's old mates among his clients. Declan actually liked the man and maybe it was his duty to warn him about Jess. And Jess about Harry. Warn them of what he wasn't sure, but he'd come up with something. Because if Jess thought she was playing around with someone else right under his nose, she was mistaken.

It didn't take much digging around to find out where Harry would be that evening. He just hoped—but somehow couldn't quite convince himself—that Jess would be pleased to see him.

• • •

As she stepped into the ladies' room, Jess pulled out her cell phone and hit speed dial. Kim picked up straightaway.

"What the hell did you put on that form?" Jess whispered as though she might be overheard.

Kim giggled. "I just described Jake. Why, what's he like?"

"Maybe not Jake, but he's gorgeous, and he's hot, and I haven't fallen asleep yet."

"That's good. You better let me know how it goes. And if you go to his place, remember—safe sex."

"Ha. And this from the woman who got pregnant the first time Jake touched her."

"Well, I'm obviously in the perfect position to give advice. And if you do go to his place, let me know so—"

"I'm not going to his place. Look I have to go. Talk to you later."

She slipped the phone back in her pocket and returned to the bar. She'd told the truth; Harry was hot, and he was interesting. But disappointingly, she felt absolutely no urge to leap on him and rip his clothes off as she always did when Declan was close. She wanted to want Harry, really she did. But there was no tingly skin, no insistent pulse between her thighs, and her heartbeat remained irritatingly slow and steady. Maybe she just needed to persevere.

She sat down opposite, took a sip of her martini, and smiled brightly. Harry was blond, his hair immaculately cut and his dark eyes held a wicked gleam as they wandered over her. She tried to imagine him in a compromising position, down an alley or in the back of a limo, but the image refused to gel in her brain.

"So tell me, Harry, why does a man like you use a dating site?"

He grinned. "A man like me?"

She studied him for a moment. He really was quite gorgeous. "You're good-looking, have a great job"—she waved a hand around their surroundings—"excellent taste."

"My job takes up most of my time. This is a good way to meet women who want the same things. And what about you? You're beautiful. I'm betting you have no problem getting dates."

She twirled her olive. "Actually, I tend to intimidate most men."

He smiled. "I'm not most men. So tell me what you like to do in your spare time, Jess."

She opened her mouth to answer something romantic and totally untrue, like walking hand in hand in the rain, when ice trickled down her spine and she snapped her lips together. She'd felt the exact same thing when she'd been in the sights of a sniper's rifle in Afghanistan. She stiffened, ready to dive for cover. Then Harry looked at someone over her shoulder. He frowned, then relaxed and smiled in welcome.

"May I join you?"

No.

The word hovered on her tongue.

"Of course," Harry said.

Traitor.

Shifting in her chair, she twisted around so she could see the man standing at her shoulder. He was wearing his usual suit, but his tie was loosened and faint stubble shadowed his jawline. Not so perfect. She liked it, and hated that she liked it. Declan's expression was bland but his eyes held humor, probably at her disgruntled expression. Behind him, Steve shifted from foot to foot, and she gave him a narrowed-eyed glare.

Declan turned and spoke quietly to him. A look of relief flashed across his face and he backed away. Taking a seat beside her and opposite Harry, Declan gave them both a charming smile. "What a coincidence. Do you come here often?"

"No," she snapped.

Harry glanced between the two of them, a small frown forming between his brows. "Do you two know each other?" She could add "not blind" and "not stupid" to Harry's list of accomplishments.

"Actually, Jess is one of my bodyguards." Declan smiled. "Dedicated to preserving my safety at all times."

"I'm off duty," she growled.

"Of course," Harry said. "I heard that you'd been shot. Have they not caught them yet?"

"Not yet. But I'm confident Jess will keep me safe." He shifted his chair a little closer, and Jess gritted her teeth.

A waitress placed a glass of scotch in front of him, and Jess took the opportunity to order another martini. She had a feeling she'd need it. Sitting back in her seat, she sipped her drink while Harry and Declan chatted about the shooting, the business, his father's birthday party, which apparently Harry had been invited to.

She jumped when Declan's free hand came to rest on her thigh and shot him her dirtiest glance, but left it there, hidden under the table. The hand slid up until it hovered at the top of her thigh and need flashed through her.

A cell phone went off. She jumped as Harry reached into his pocket, pulled out a phone, and read the screen. "I have to take this."

"What a pity," Declan murmured. "I'll look after Jess for you."

Harry cast him an amused glance. "I'm sure you will. I'll be right back," he added to her, and she watched as he strolled out of the bar, phone held to his ear.

Declan squeezed her leg.

"Did you arrange that?" she asked.

"The phone call? No, *that* was purely good luck."

"But you admit this is no coincidence. And how come you didn't mention you know Harry?"

"I thought I'd surprise you." He shrugged and looked around them. "At least Harry's got some class."

"What are you doing here, Declan?"

"Just passing."

"Yeah, right."

He removed his hand, and turned in his chair so he was facing her. Beneath the amusement, anger flickered in his eyes. "Absolutely nothing is going to happen between you and Harry. So don't pretend otherwise."

"And why's that?"

"Because you're mine. You're just too stubborn to admit it." He gave her a long slow look and all of a sudden her skin was tingly and that pulse was beating frantically between her thighs.

She hated that. Why was he the one man who could do this to her? Why couldn't Harry have made her all tingly? Was Declan hardwired into her system? But no way was she his. And no way did she want to be. But how to convince Declan of that.

She shifted her chair so she could watch him as she spoke. "I've been thinking this through," she said. "You want to keep me around because you're bored with your perfect life and I make you feel alive. But I won't be used like that."

His brows drew together. "It wouldn't be using you."

"No? If there's something wrong with your life, Declan, you need to work out what and make some changes. Not just keep doing the same shit and having sex with me to brighten up the dull moments." She pushed her chair back and stood up. "I'm leaving. I'll say my good-byes to Harry on the way out."

For a second, she thought he would try and stop her, but then he sat back. "Okay, I'll let you go…this time. But Jess, be in no doubt. While you might not be ready to accept you're mine, you're certainly not going to be any other man's. Forget the dates."

She wanted to say *or else*? But decided, maybe this time, discretion was a better idea. She turned around and walked away, his eyes burning into her back the whole way out.

Chapter Eleven

"Are you avoiding me?" Declan lounged back in his big leather seat, but he felt far from relaxed. His hand gripped the phone, his fingers tightening at the silence on the other end of the call.

"Yes," she finally answered.

He hadn't seen her alone in the five days since he'd gate-crashed her date with Harry. She kept to her word, and she was part of the job; she'd accompanied him to two dinners in the last week, and she'd been the perfect girlfriend as long as she was in company. But she always managed to slip away before he could maneuver her somewhere alone. And the guys followed her like hawks. They were doing a better job guarding her than they were him.

He was pissed off and frustrated as hell. And he couldn't get her words out of his head. Did he need to work out what was wrong with his life? Was there even anything wrong? Or was everything fucking wrong? He didn't know anymore.

"Are you going to tell me why?" he asked.

She was silent for a long time.

"Jess?"

"Sorry, just working out what to say to make you bugger off and leave me the hell alone."

"Why not go ahead and try. I'll tell you if it's working."

"Hmm… How about it was fun for a while, but rehashing old affairs never really works."

"And how would you know that. Have you extensive experience?"

"Enough."

The strange thing was he was pretty sure she had very little experience. She'd been a virgin when she'd first gone with him. He could still remember the surprise that had dealt him. She'd been so wild, even though she'd been only seventeen. She'd dressed like a tart and mixed with an older crowd. He'd just presumed.

Back then she never talked about her family. He'd guessed they were fairly well off; she'd been attending private school. And when he'd met her sister that had been confirmed, though Jess and her sister had seemed almost like different species.

So why had she been the way she was? What had made her crave danger? She'd pushed him and pushed him as though she needed to see how far he would allow her to go.

Why did he suddenly feel like he had let her down all those years ago?

"Declan, you still there? Or did it work."

"So you're bored with the sex?"

"Yeah."

She was lying.

But why?

"Come here and tell me that to my face."

"Thanks for the invite, but I think I'll pass."

"You can't avoid me forever."

"I think I can." She was silent for a moment. "Anyway, after tomorrow night the trial will begin, and once you've given evidence, then this whole thing will be over."

It would never be over. He knew that now. He just needed to convince Jess of that. She was definitely running scared, but he wasn't sure exactly what she feared.

Trusting him again, obviously. He'd let her down. But he suspected it was more than that.

"Come over tonight," he said. "We can talk."

"We have nothing to say. Besides, I can't. Girls' night out." And she broke the connection.

· · ·

Okay, so she shouldn't be here. It was over.

Jess had been doing a great job of avoiding Declan, but since that phone call earlier, she hadn't been able to settle.

She'd convinced herself that the only way she was going to convince him that she was serious about the no-more-sex thing was face-to-face.

Delusional or what?

But somehow she had found herself out on the street, hailing a cab and giving the address of Declan's office to the cabbie. And now here she was, sitting in reception, trying to give herself a stern talking to about the meaning of face-to-face, and how it did not mean chest to chest or pelvis to pelvis.

Or she had been doing until one minute ago when the

elevator doors slid open and Declan had emerged. With a woman. A very beautiful, smart-looking woman, who he ushered out of the elevator with a hand at her waist. Now he was standing by the reception desk, leaning in toward her, listening to something she was saying, a small smile on his face. He obviously knew her well; it was there in the body language.

Steve and Rick, today's bodyguards, had followed him out, keeping a discreet distance. Jess scowled as she caught Steve's gaze and shook her head slightly.

Maybe now wasn't the time to do the face-to-face thing. Maybe now was the time to work out what the hell was going on in her brain.

Because her first inclination was to head over there and rip that woman's hand away from Declan's arm. Then probably drop-kick her to the ground and tear out her perfectly styled hair.

And that was way beyond rational.

She was in so much trouble.

The thing was, she didn't actually believe there was anything going on between Declan and Ms. Perfect. But that was beside the point. She had this voice screaming in her head.

Mine. Mine. Mine.

And Declan wasn't hers. And more to the point, she really didn't want him to be hers. She was supposed to be getting him out of her system once and for all. Not going all manic possessive.

She'd thought he was hers once before and look how well that had turned out. She had a flash of remembered pain, and then the memories flooded over her. The rage and sense of powerlessness that there was absolutely nothing she could do to make him stay. The knowledge that she would have done just about anything for one more night in his arms. How much she had needed him after the accident, and he hadn't been there for her. She'd even swallowed her pride and gone running after him. Only to find him gone. She *wouldn't* go through that again.

A movement from her left dragged her gaze away from the couple. Rory McCabe. He sank into the chair beside her. "Good afternoon, Jessica. You look a little tense."

She shrugged. "Not at all. Just checking in."

He waved a hand toward where Declan stood his head bent over the woman. "That's Penny."

Why did that name sound familiar? "Penny as in Declan's ex-fiancée Penny?"

He grinned. "Yes. From the look on your face, you were thinking about taking her out. But she's no threat."

Did those words have a double meaning? Why had Rory thrown her and Declan together again after all these years? Would he tell her if she asked?

"They look perfect together," she said just to find out what he thought about the other woman.

He snorted. "Yeah, they look like a couple of perfect corporate…robots."

She let out a small laugh, loud enough to be heard across the way, but Declan was obviously engrossed and his head didn't lift from where it was bent low over Penny the ex.

"He knows you're here," Rory said.

"How do you work that out?" He seemed oblivious to everyone but the woman in front of him.

"Because he's never been that attentive to Penny in his entire life."

She dragged her gaze away from Declan to study his father. In some ways, he was so like Declan; in others, he was completely different. Rory had deep lines of experience—and laughter—etched into his face. His dark eyes looked like they had seen the worst the world could throw at him. And they probably had. But she suspected the two men were more similar than appearances suggested. It was just their lives had led them in different directions. Suddenly she needed to understand just what had brought her and Declan together again after all these years. "What are you after?" she asked.

"After?" He sounded so innocent. Except Rory McCabe didn't have an innocent cell in his body.

"Come on, Rory, you can tell me," she coaxed. "Why did you employ me to protect Declan? You could have employed another company. We're good, but there are others just as good."

He pursed his lips and looked at Declan and Penny. He was leaning against the wall now, seemingly totally absorbed in his ex-fiancé. "Because I love my son." He turned back to her. "You might not believe it, but I did my best to split you up all those years ago because I thought it was the best thing for Declan."

She reached across and patted his arm. "Don't fret about it. I'd already come to the conclusion that we would have been hell together. It wouldn't have taken us long. You just sped things up."

"Maybe. Maybe not."

He was so damn cryptic. "You know I hate you." She glanced back at Declan. "Both of you."

He chuckled. "Yeah, I know. But let me tell you something about our family and maybe you'll hate Declan a little less. And understand him a little more."

Jess knew she should get up and tell Rory McCabe that she had no interest in understanding his son any more than she did now. But she didn't move.

Rory stretched his long legs out in front of him and settled in his chair. "My father came over from Ireland after the Second World War and literally carved himself a place in the East End of London. Gambling, prostitution, later on drugs—he didn't mind where the money came from. And he didn't care who he stepped on in the process."

"Sounds like a nice guy."

"Not even vaguely. He was killed in a revenge attack when I was twenty-one, and I took over the business."

"I bet that was hard."

"Yeah. It was also a whole lot of fun. I did what I wanted, when I wanted, and trampled over anyone who stood in my way."

"Nice."

"'Nice' it was not, but I was just a kid. A lot of people wanted to see me go down, so I had to toughen up fast."

"So what changed you?"

"First Logan came along. His mother and I didn't last, and she made it as hard as possible for me to see him."

"Declan said you got custody when Logan was ten."

He looked her over. "So you've talked about this stuff with Declan."

"Not really. Just in passing, when it touched on the job."

"Oh yes, the 'job.' Anyway, Logan was already a total tearaway even at ten, not much hope keeping him on the straight and narrow. By then I'd met and married Declan's mother. Christ she was"—he shook his head—"different.

And I wanted her, but she'd only have me if I went straight."

"Aw, the love of a good woman."

He laughed, and this time, across the way, Declan lifted his head and gave the two of them a narrow-eyed stare. So Rory had been right—Declan was quite aware of her presence. Could he actually be trying to make her jealous?

"I'm not sure I'd ever classify Judith as a 'good woman.' But she had determination. She was a perfectionist, and I was far from perfect and too set in my ways to change enough to satisfy her. But by the time Declan came along I knew I didn't want a son of mine living the same life I had. Always looking over his shoulder, expecting the cops to be behind him. Worrying that his kids would get caught up in some mess and end up inside."

"So the two of you decided Declan was going to be a 'good' boy."

"He was a good boy." He grinned. "It's in his genes."

"Right. Of course it is."

"But yeah, we might have drummed it in a little hard that he had a duty, couldn't afford to play up, get attention. Plus, just when he got to a troublesome age, Logan got put away. Declan blamed himself."

"Why would he do that?"

"Because Logan got Declan out of a fight and stayed behind to teach them a lesson for picking on his little brother. The police broke up the fight and one of the coppers accidentally got slugged in the face…by Logan."

"Oh. Nasty." Poor Declan.

"After that Declan didn't give us any trouble. The perfect son." He sounded almost sad at the notion. "Though he did ask for a Harley for his eighteenth birthday."

"Did you get him one?" He certainly hadn't had a Harley when she'd known him, she would have noticed.

"No, I got him a Porsche."

"Figures." She couldn't believe she felt sorry for someone for getting a Porsche for a present.

But really, what difference did this insight make? This conversation might have made her understand a little better why Declan was the way he was, and also why he'd dumped her all those years ago. But she'd already guessed a lot of it. She'd been leading him off the straight and narrow, but she reckoned she wasn't trying to take him anywhere he didn't really want to go deep down. It was the whole nature versus nurture thing. They'd brought Declan up to be well behaved, good, and to subdue his wilder nature, but that didn't mean it wasn't still there underneath, simmering away.

"I still don't get it," she said. "Why the meddling? Why aren't you and…Judith really pleased with the way he's turned out? He's…perfect."

"We want him to be happy."

"And he isn't?"

"He's going through the motions. And he's ready to explode."

She looked away, back to Declan who now stood in profile. So he could keep an eye on them? He seemed outwardly relaxed, but if she looked closely she could see a tic working in his cheek and his fingers flexing at his side. He glanced across and caught her gaze. A shiver of something—apprehension or anticipation, she wasn't sure which—ran through her.

Was he really on the point of exploding? And did she want to be around if that happened? But then he'd always given the impression of leashed power, of trouble locked tightly inside; it was what had drawn her to him. What had made her push and push at those locks to see if she could get to the real Declan.

Another shiver. This one settled low down in her belly.

Maybe it was time to get out of there. She could leave the whole no-more-sex conversation until another time. When she'd convinced herself that it was really the only option.

She pushed herself to her feet. Rory was watching her through narrowed eyes. "Too much of a coward to risk the explosion?" he murmured.

"Hell yes!" She whirled around and stalked away.

· · ·

"You know she's going to give me shit assignments for this for the rest of eternity," Steve muttered from behind him, where he was guarding Declan's back along with his other bodyguard for the night. They hadn't been happy with his change of plans, but he'd insisted.

After much persuasion, Steve had finally given up Jess's location. The alternative had been to troll the bars and clubs until Declan found her. Obviously, Steve had decided risking Jess's ire was the lesser of two evils. As acting head of the company, she had to be reachable at all times, but it turned out that Steve had overheard her arranging the night out at the office earlier in the day.

"And you know," Steve added, "this could be classified as serious stalking."

"I'll tell her you had no choice," Declan replied.

The bar was just off the embankment. Steps led downward into a basement. Tables were scattered around the floor area, but most people were standing. It was Saturday night and the place was buzzing. He stood for a moment adjusting to the dim light, then searched the room.

He spotted her almost immediately. Her back was to him, but as he stared, her shoulders stiffened. But she didn't turn and he headed toward her.

She was with two other women, a tall, stunning brunette with crimson streaks in her dark hair and a tiny redhead, with a cute face and huge green eyes. They were both facing him and looked up as he came to a halt beside the table. Jess still didn't turn.

"I take it you're Declan, the prick," the redhead murmured.

He wondered how many people had seen that damn tattoo.

Finally, Jess turned around slowly. She ignored Declan and spoke to Steve. "You are so fucked."

"Yeah, I reckon." But he grinned. "Me and Rick are going to go sit over there at a safe distance and keep an eye on things. You two play nice."

Declan waited until his two babysitters had melted into the drinkers and then sat himself down in the empty seat across from Jess and next to the redhead.

"I'm Dani," she said.

"And I'm Kim," the brunette offered. "And we're going to go to the bar and get some more drinks."

They both stood in unison. Declan waited for Jess to tell them to stay, or more likely tell him to go, but she remained silent and the two girls disappeared, leaving them alone.

She looked tired and heartbreakingly beautiful. Dressed simply in jeans, boots, and a black T-shirt, her hair pulled into a ponytail, her face clean of makeup. She was turned slightly away so he couldn't see the scar, and for a moment she looked so like her seventeen-year-old self that his heart missed a beat.

Someone put some music on in the background; he recognized the song. It was one they had danced to all those years ago, through the long hot summer nights.

She recognized it as well and for a second, a slight smile curled her bottom lip and then was gone.

"I still hear certain songs and they take me back to that summer, scents, places in the city…" he said softly.

"Yeah," she replied. "Memories are a bummer. Wouldn't it be great if we could just wipe them out and start over?"

One hand was wrapped around her bottle of beer, and Declan reached across and uncurled her fingers, slid her palm into his. She didn't try to pull away, but a slight frown formed between her arched brows.

"I would never wipe away the memory of that summer with you," he said and he knew he spoke the truth. However painful the aftermath, he would still rather have the pleasure and the pain. "Those months with you will always be the best of my life."

He waited for her to make a smart comeback, but she remained silent, gnawing on her lower lip and gazing at the spot where their hands joined.

He stroked her palm with the pad of his thumb and a shiver ran through her.

"Why have you been avoiding me?" he asked. "I missed you."

Her frown deepened, and she studied his face. "Why are you being so nice? Why can't you go back to being a prick?"

"I am nice." He picked up her hand, brought it to his mouth, uncurled her fingers and placed a kiss in the center of his palm. "Don't you think I'm nice?"

She looked away for long moments. "No, actually I don't. But I don't think it matters whether you're nice or not. I hate you, remember?"

"Maybe. But ten years is a long time to hate, and I think you're tired of hating me."

She shook her head. "I don't know what you want here, Declan. Absolution? If so, then you have it. You're absolved. I forgive you for dumping me."

"Maybe I want another chance."

Shock flared on her face, darkening her eyes to midnight, and she tugged at the hold of his hand.

He held on tight. "I know you feel something."

She sat back in her seat, her gaze flicking over him. "Okay, you want the truth. Yes, I feel something and that's the very reason why I'm going to finish this job and then I'm going to get as far away as I can from you."

"What happened to facing your fears? I never thought you were a coward."

"Well, maybe you never really knew me." She took a deep breath. "You obviously want a good honest heart-to-heart, get things out in the open. So okay, here's how it is. Ten years ago you broke me."

He winced. At the same time, he was surprised that she would admit that much. Her hand was still in his, and he tightened his grip on her as though she might bolt. "You always seemed so strong."

"Maybe I'm a good actress. Oh, it wasn't all your fault, I was a mess before I met you and—"

"Why? What happened to you? You never talked about yourself back then."

She shrugged, and he was sure she wasn't going to open up, then she started talking fast, "My parents died when I was ten. I wasn't really over it when I met you. I blamed myself. They were doctors, working for a charity in Zambia. They took me with them and I loved it. But then I got ill. Malaria. They died in a small plane crash taking me to hospital. I was the only survivor."

"Hardly your fault."

"Oh logically I know that, but we don't see things so clearly when we're young."

"I'm sorry."

"Don't be, I'm over it. But my point is you were the first person I allowed in, the first person I trusted, the only person I allowed myself to love after they died. And you let me down."

"I know." He ran a hand through his hair.

"I thought we had something special. Hell, I *know* we had something special. And you just walked away like I didn't matter."

"You mattered."

"Not enough."

This was killing him. He hadn't expected her to be so open, and he had no clue how to deal with it. Also, despite her honesty, there was a sense of separateness to her as if she was already distancing herself. He had an inkling this wasn't leading up to any sort of let's-forgive-and-forget-and-fall-in-love-again statement. And that wasn't how he wanted the evening to end.

"So you see," she said, "whatever I feel for you now, whatever I think we could have is irrelevant because I just don't want it. Yes, you're a great fuck and no man has ever made me feel the way you do, but I will not allow myself to fall in love with you again. I won't allow you to break me again."

"We're different people now, Jess. We were kids. Things won't be the same this time."

"No, they won't because I won't allow them to be. I'm not sure why you've had this change of heart, but really it doesn't matter. You walked away last time. Walk away again."

"I can't."

"Then I will." She tugged her hand free and this time he let her go. Rising to her feet, she stared across at him.

Declan pushed back his chair and stood up. No way was she walking out of here without him. "You said until the job was over. We have two more nights, Jess."

"You still want to sleep with me?"

"Hell, yes."

. . .

She was drained from all the confessional stuff and from fighting her need for him. At the same time, she felt strangely clearheaded. As though setting it all out for Declan had made it clear to her as well.

Yes, she was a coward.

But it was a matter of self-preservation. He was a weakness ingrained in her character. Where Declan was concerned, she was all or nothing. She wouldn't risk all again. So she had to accept nothing.

But being in contact with Declan and not touching him was driving her insane. How close had she come earlier today to giving in, giving them both what they wanted? What they needed.

Once this job was over, she would never see him again. It would take time to get over him, to forget, but she would do it. She was strong.

In the meantime, why fight it?

As she gave in, a wave of weakness washed over her and she reached out and rested a hand against the tabletop.

"Let me take you home," Declan said.

She gave a quick nod and then searched the room. She found Kim and Dani leaning against the bar, drinks in hand, watching her. "Give me a minute," she said to Declan and walked across to where they stood.

"So have you kissed and made up?" Kim said.

"Not exactly."

"You know he likes you," Dani added. "He's watching you now. He doesn't take his eyes off you."

"Like a stalker," Jess suggested, glancing across to where he stood. He looked so beautiful tonight, more like she remembered him from all those years ago. Still in his suit, but his tie was gone and his shirt open at the throat. His perfect image was unraveling. "I'm going to take a rain check on tonight," she said. "Declan and I have things to…talk about."

"Of course you do." Kim leaned across and kissed her on the cheek. "Call us if you need us."

Jess nodded and headed back to Declan. They didn't talk as they made their way out of the bar and onto the street. She was vaguely aware of Declan's bodyguards following them, but they kept their distance.

It was only ten minutes' walk to her flat, one of the reasons they usually met at that particular bar, and they strolled along in silence not touching. She let them into the ground floor flat and then peered through the window. Steve was outside on the street, leaning against the wall. The other man was nowhere in sight, probably looking around the area. It was weird being on the other side of the bodyguard thing, but then she pushed them from her mind again and turned her attention to Declan.

He wandered around the small sitting room, lightly touching things as he passed. The place wasn't much, but it was hers. She'd bought it outright with money her parents had left her. It was small but in a convenient location.

She shrugged out of her jacket and tossed it onto the sofa. "You want a drink?" she asked Declan.

He shook his head. "I want you."

She forced her lips into a smile. "Well, you can have me. For one more day." She thought he was going to argue, spoil things, and she wanted this, didn't want to make him leave. She held up a hand. "No more talking. We've said enough."

She turned around and headed out of the room, down the hall to her bedroom. Declan followed her in and the door closed. After reaching into his pocket, he pulled out a handful of condoms and tossed them on the bedside table. She hadn't realized how small the room was, most of the floor space taken up by the huge bed. She liked to sprawl.

She strolled around the bed, tugging her T-shirt over her head on the way. She toed off her boots and then stripped off her jeans leaving her in a plain black bra and panties. His eyes were fixed on her as she reached behind her and unclasped her bra, then pushed the panties down over her long legs and stepped out of them to stand before him naked. She pulled the band that tied her hair loose so it fell around her shoulders and she ran a hand over her scalp easing the tension.

He hadn't moved, his gaze intent as it roamed over her body. "You're so beautiful."

She stepped toward him, her fingers trembling as they flicked open the buttons of his shirt. After dragging it down over his shoulders, she ran her palm over the satin skin of his chest, scraping over the nipples to come to rest on his belt. She opened it with fumbling fingers. Heat and need were building inside her, concentrating at her breasts and between her thighs. Finally the belt came undone, and she flicked open the fastener and lowered the zipper.

He took over then, pushing the pants and boxers down over his long legs, kicking off his shoes, until he too was naked. And so beautiful, he made her chest ache. Her gaze ran down over his lean ridged belly, then lower. He was already fully erect, his shaft vertical against his stomach, long and thick, pulsating under her stare.

His hand cupped her around the back of her neck, drew her the last few inches that kept them apart. Every nerve tingled, every inch of skin prickling with need.

Usually the sex was hard and fast, as though they had a point to make, but from the first gentle touch of his lips, she knew tonight would be different.

He took her mouth with long, slow, wet kisses, angling her head so his lips slanted over hers, his tongue filling her, stroking her everywhere, her lips, her teeth, the sensitive roof of her mouth, until her head fell back and she allowed him to do as he would.

"So beautiful." He slid his hands down to her waist and picked her up. For a second he held her cradled against his chest, then he lowered her to the mattress, coming down beside her. "I need to be inside you so much. I've been going mad these last few days, seeing you, not touching you."

She watched as he tore open a condom packet and rolled it down over his erection. His hands skimmed down over her body, tracing the shape, as if fixing it in his memory. She kept her eyes open because she didn't want to miss a second of this, even when he kissed her again and she could see the black ring around his silver irises, the faint shadow of stubble on his cheek.

He shifted to lie over her, his weight balanced on his elbows, one knee pressing between her thighs, widening her legs. She felt the broad head of his cock, scalding hot, push between the folds of her sex, sliding against the slippery wetness until it found the entrance to her body and hovered there. She shifted her hips, restless for more, and he pushed in just a little bit farther. Then he sighed and sank his length into her, filling her completely.

She'd always played an active part during sex, but now she lay immobile, absorbing the sensations washing through her. The exquisite drag of his cock as he pulled out, the delicious friction as he shoved back in, the almost unbearable pleasure as he ground against her clit with each stroke. He wasn't touching her anywhere else now, just gazing down into her eyes, his expression almost tortured.

Tingles were spreading through her body, swirling, coalescing. She could sense the slow, inexorable buildup of pleasure, knew he felt it as well in the tightening of his muscles, but still he kept his strokes slow and steady, until she was shifting restlessly under him, reaching for her release.

His mouth opened, but she didn't want words and she wrapped a hand around his neck, pulled him down for a kiss.

Finally, his spine arched and he came, pulsing inside her,

grinding against her, tipping her over the edge, so the pleasure swelled and burst, shattering her into a million pieces.

Long minutes later, he flung himself onto his side and pulled her hard against him, curving his big body around hers, fitting her against him. Just a few minutes and she'd tell him to leave. But the sleepless nights caught up with her, and wrapped in his arms, she drifted off into sleep. She had no clue how much later it was when she woke again to waves of pleasure undulating through her body. Declan was still behind her, one big hand cupped her breast, rubbing the nipple, the other was between her legs. One finger was inside, stroking her inner walls while the pad of his thumb traced lazy circles over her clit. As if he sensed she was awake, he increased the pressure, pushing another finger inside, massaging the swollen bud. She didn't fight the swell of pleasure, just let it wash over her in warm, delicious waves.

While she still pulsated from her orgasm, he withdrew his hand, lifted her thigh, and pushed into her from behind. She gasped as he filled her, then gave herself over to the pleasure. His fingers tugged at her nipples, pinching and then soothing, while his mouth and tongue traced wet patterns on her neck and her shoulders.

As the tension built, he touched her lightly between the thighs and she came again, feeling his cock swell, then pulse with his own release.

She lay, half beside him, half beneath him. Some inner sense was warning her that she needed to move, but this felt so perfect, so right and instead, she pushed back against him as he wrapped his arms around her.

"I love you." The declaration whispered across her skin, sank into her mind, and she had to blink back the tears.

At least he couldn't see the effect his words had on her. Because if he did, she doubted she would ever make him go, and suddenly she needed him gone.

Because she could feel herself cracking and breaking all over again.

She wiped all expression from her face, pulled herself free, and sat up, wrapping her arms around her knees. "It's time for you to go."

Shock flared in his face, followed by a flash of anger. "Are you telling me you feel nothing?"

She bit her lip. "Didn't you listen to a word I said earlier? It doesn't matter what I feel. I won't allow this to go any further. I can't." Maybe it was time for those tears after all. She blinked, allowed one to roll down over her cheek and he almost recoiled in horror.

"Jess?"

She sniffed.

"I did this to you? Talk to me."

She swallowed. Maybe it was time to tell him the rest. "Did you ever wonder why I was coming to see you that night? The night I had the accident."

"I presumed you were just coming to try and patch things up."

"I was pregnant."

His face went blank. "What?"

"Only a few weeks, but I'd taken at least three tests." And God, she'd been so happy, thrilled, excited at the thought of Declan's baby. She'd known he would do the right thing, wouldn't abandon them, and by that point she would have done anything to get him back. She didn't want to be that person again.

"What happened?"

"I lost it." And only then had she realized how much she had desperately wanted the baby and not just as a means of keeping Declan.

"In the accident?"

"Maybe. But the doctor said it might have happened anyway. It does sometimes, and it was so early, just a handful of cells."

"Why didn't you tell me?"

"I didn't know about the miscarriage when you visited. I was still in shock from the accident. Then you said it was over…again. And I realized I wanted you to stay because you wanted *me* and not because it was the right thing to do. But after I got out of hospital, I was hurting and I needed you so badly. I would have even accepted the friendship thing at that point. I was so pathetic."

"And I was gone."

"You were. I saw Rory and he basically told me to take the hint and leave you alone. Anyway, I had no way of contacting you so I decided to take his advice. But it hurt. So excuse me if I don't want to lay myself open to that again."

"It wouldn't—"

But she'd had enough. "Please go, Declan. Please. I can't take any more."

He looked at her for an age longer, then gave a brisk nod of his head. "I'll go, as long as you promise you'll come tomorrow night."

Tomorrow night was his father's birthday, and there was to be a big party at the club. The last night before Declan was due to give evidence at the trial. And then this would all be over.

"I'll be there."

He rolled to his feet, raked a hand through his hair—it was growing longer—he hadn't had it cut since they'd met again, and now it tousled over his forehead. Naked, he was spectacular, and she didn't try to look away. Would she ever see him like this again? The thought that this might be the last time was like a black cloud engulfing her mind. But that only made her more determined to get out before she went beyond the point of turning back.

He picked up his clothes, and dragged them on, sat on the edge of the bed to pull on his shoes, and then his gaze fixed on something on her wall.

She followed the look and her breath caught in her throat. Declan rose slowly to his feet and took a step closer, then reached out and unhooked the frame from the wall, examined it closely.

"My father gave you this?"

"That day I went to see him. It doesn't matter anymore."

He gave her a look as if to say she was crazy. "You've had this for over ten years, you put it on your goddamned bedroom wall, and you say it doesn't matter."

She had no clue how to answer. Unfortunately Declan wasn't quite so reticent.

He shook his head. "I can't believe he gave you this." He waved the check in her face.

"He was doing what he thought was right for you."

He gritted his teeth. "How the fucking hell dare you defend him?" He pulled the frame apart, took out the check, and tucked it into his back pocket. "Just make sure you're there tomorrow night. Or I'll come looking."

And he was gone.

Chapter Twelve

Declan hovered outside the bedroom door, unsure whether to go back in. But his brain was about to explode. And he needed out of there before that happened, causing who knew what damage.

Except for that one brief interlude with Jess, all his life, he'd kept his emotions under rigid control. Not allowed himself to feel, done his goddamned fucking duty. Done what his father expected of him.

Now that control was slipping away.

She'd been seventeen years old and pregnant with his baby. And he'd walked away. She'd had a miscarriage and endured it alone. Because he'd been too much of a pussy to go after what he wanted.

He couldn't believe his own father had given Jess money to leave him alone. Except who was he kidding? His father was a ruthless bastard. Always had been. But it was hardly his father's fault—well not all of it. *He'd* been the one to walk. But he wouldn't do that a second time, no matter what she believed she wanted.

She made him feel alive. She was the only thing that ever had and his life since had been gray and meaningless. A performance he put on for the rest of the world. Only Jess saw through it.

She'd been right the other night when she'd told him he needed to change. He just wasn't sure how. Maybe he needed to take a leap into the unknown. And he'd be happy to do that with Jess at his side.

He glanced back at the door, but then turned away.

He'd told her he loved her.

He'd never said that to any woman except Jess.

And she said it didn't matter. But it was all that mattered. And she meant what she said. She really planned to finish this thing between them.

He had to leave, give her some space. Think about what he could do to make her give him a chance. Maybe he should steal a car. Take her joyriding. Get them both locked up. Or maybe not.

But right now she had worked herself up, put an insurmountable barrier between them, which she wouldn't let him pass. He could only hope that she would think about his words.

He had one more day to persuade her.

He headed out, slamming the front door behind him. The night was cold and he shivered as Steve fell into step behind him.

"Is she all right?" he asked, his voice expressionless. Declan had gotten the distinct impression that Jess's colleagues didn't approve of their relationship.

"Why the hell wouldn't she be all right?" he snarled. What did they think he was going to do to her? Break her heart?

Steve shrugged. "She's been different since this job. We just don't want her hurt."

He stopped and swung around. "And you think I'll do that?" He fisted his hands at his side, resisting the urge to punch the other man.

Steve shrugged again, then obviously decided he'd said enough. "You want me to call for a car?"

"No." He didn't want to head home. He wanted a drink. He started walking, heading toward the center of town, and then into the first bar he found.

He ordered a scotch, drank it in one swallow, then ordered another and took it to a dark corner. Drank that. When he raised his glass, the barman came over, this time he filled the glass and left the bottle on the table.

She hadn't actually said she didn't love him.

Maybe he needed to give her some concrete evidence that he really did care, and this time he meant it to last. The scotch was a warm buzz in his brain now.

He pushed himself to his feet and headed over to where Steve waited and watched.

"I want to hit something," he said. Actually, he wanted to hit his father, but he reckoned he'd better postpone that confrontation until he was a little calmer and a little more sober. "Do you have any suggestions?"

Half an hour later, Declan sagged against the punching bag, resting his forehead against the soft leather. They were in a room beneath the Knight Securities building, next to the shooting range where he'd made love with Jess. He was trying not to think about that. He lifted his head. His bodyguard leaned against the wall, one eyebrow raised. "You done?"

"Not nearly done. Do you know of a tattoo place open at this time?"

• • •

It was hardly daylight when Jess entered the Knight Security building the following morning. She'd checked his schedule and knew Jake was around and she wanted to do this before she changed her mind.

She hadn't slept after Declan had left.

She'd lain in bed, trying to avoid thinking about him, because it hurt. Instead, she'd thought about everything else. Her parents, who had been the most wonderful people and hadn't deserved to die. Her sister, who had very reluctantly taken her in and had been totally unprepared to deal with a damaged, hurting ten-year-old. The army, her job, her future...

And she realized something. Declan wasn't the only one who didn't know what he wanted. Except she knew what she didn't want and that was to spend the rest of her life trying to be something she wasn't. Like nice.

She'd thought the promotion was everything she wanted, but in fact it would be a combination of all the parts of the job she hated. Administration, paperwork, getting friendly with clients. It was the hands-on work she loved. Designing security systems, training the operatives, field work. She'd die of boredom stuck in an office all day.

All the same, she'd never found it easy to admit she was wrong. Even to herself.

Taking a deep breath, she knocked on the door and

pushed it open. Jake was seated on the sofa, drinking coffee, working on his laptop.

"Can we talk?" she said.

He gestured to the seat opposite. "What is it?"

She settled herself, then jumped up, crossed to the coffee, poured one, and came back. After taking a sip, she exhaled. "I think you should give the job to Gary."

Jake put his cup down and studied her. "Why?"

"Because I don't want to be nice. I've tried it, and it *really* doesn't suit me."

His lips twitched. Then he shrugged. "Okay."

"Okay?" She frowned. "Hey, boss, this is the moment you're supposed to try and dissuade me. Tell me the firm needs me. That I'm better than Gary…"

"You are. But actually, I think you're making the right decision."

"You do."

"You could do the job, but you'd come to hate it in the end. And you're bright enough to realize that."

"Aw, thanks."

"So what will you do?"

"Hey, I worked out what I don't want. Could you give me a little time to sort out the hard stuff?"

He nodded. "You'll get there. Just remember what you are. It will help you decide."

"And what am I?"

He grinned. "A fucking badass."

• • •

The bouncer was a man named Pete. The same man who

had guarded his room after the shooting. Declan had known him most of his life. Pete did a double take as he opened the door and then nodded as Declan walked passed, his two bodyguards close behind him.

"Are they all here?" he asked.

"Yeah," Pete said. "They're in your old man's office. Just waiting for you to start the celebrations."

Declan walked through the club. It was only eight and still quiet. That wouldn't last for long. He didn't bother knocking on the office door, just pushed it open. Leaving his guards outside the door, he stepped inside.

His dad sat behind the big desk, feet resting on the polished wood, legs crossed at the ankles, arms behind his head. He raised an eyebrow when he saw Declan, but didn't make any comment.

There were four other people in the room, the whole family together. He didn't think he'd seen his father and mother in the same room for at least five years. They dealt much better together when there was an ocean between them. There was also his sister and brother, and Penny, his ex-fiancé, who was eying him up as though he'd metamorphosed into something dangerous.

They'd never been what you would consider a functioning family unit. But he loved them. Even his bastard of a father. Even if he didn't like him much right now—and that was a total understatement.

"Looking good, Bro," Logan drawled, a grin curling his lips.

Logan had been his role model for tonight. A few years older than Declan, he'd been born before the urge to be respectable had overtaken Rory and he'd never really embraced the whole legitimate thing. But Declan knew he was a good man, even if he looked a total hard case in black leather pants and a T-shirt, the short sleeves revealing the black ink of tattoos snaking down his arms. Declan's own arm tingled at the sight.

His sister, Tamara, was the opposite, looking every inch the successful corporate lawyer she was. She was two years younger and very ambitious. She been hassling him for more responsibility. He was about to make her very happy.

He took off his dark glasses and shoved them in his pocket, wincing a little at the bright light. "Stand up," he said to his dad.

Rory frowned but slowly rose to his feet. Declan closed the distance between them. "Tell me," he said. "Did you really have a heart attack last year, or was it just part of the plot to get me over here and sort out my pitiful existence?"

He pursed his lips. "My heart's fine."

"Good." He drew back his fist and punched his father in the nose.

He heard the satisfying crunch of bone and Rory crashed to the floor.

Declan looked around the room, waiting for someone to step forward, but no one moved. Logan was still grinning, his sister looked uninterested, his mother was smiling.

"I have wanted to do that so many times," she murmured. Then she stepped toward him and patted his arm. "Do you two need to talk alone?"

Declan shook his head. "No. I can say what I have to say in front of you."

"Good." She drifted away and sat down in the middle of the black leather sofa that ran along one wall of the office.

She tapped the seat beside her and Logan and Tamara sat on either side. Penny raised an eyebrow, then shook her head. "I'm guessing this is a family matter, so I'll leave you to it." Declan waited until she had closed the door behind her before he turned back.

His dad hadn't yet moved and for a moment Declan worried that he might have hit too hard. But he'd pulled the punch. Then Rory pushed himself up onto one elbow and wiped a hand across his nose, staring at the scarlet that stained his fingers. "You broke my nose."

"Yeah."

He dragged himself to his feet. "Are you going to tell me why?"

Declan reached into his pocket and pulled out the check he had taken from Jess's wall last night. He tossed it onto the desk beside where his father stood.

He picked it up, his brows drawing together as he studied the check. Then his expression cleared though his eyes narrowed. "She never cashed it?" He sounded almost pleased.

What the hell did that matter? "She came to you, and you gave her money to go away."

"She was bad for you."

"It wasn't your decision to make. You promised to let me know if she needed anything. I asked you if she'd been in touch. You lied."

"I made it my decision. You were only eighteen and about to throw your future away on a little tramp."

"She was never a tramp." Declan turned away, running a hand through his hair. He would never get his father to admit he was wrong. Arrogant prick. "You should have fucking told me."

Rory pursed his lips. "Maybe. But if you'd really wanted her back then, you would never have left."

Declan crossed to the cabinet where he knew his father kept the scotch and pulled out the bottle and a couple of glasses. He placed them on the desk.

"Don't we get offered any?" Logan asked.

"Get it yourself." He poured an inch into each and handed one to his father, who eyed him suspiciously, but took the glass and swallowed the drink.

"You going to hit me again?"

"Maybe." But he sank down into the chair opposite his father's, legs stretched out in front of him, and sipped the drink while he examined his new boots. There was more he wanted to know and if he had to beat the answers out of his father, well, he was willing to do it. But he didn't think it would come to that.

"Why did you employ Knight Security? And why did you specifically ask for Jess?"

His father swirled the amber liquid around in his glass while he considered the answer. Why did Declan get the impression that whatever it was he wasn't going to like it?"

But it was his mother who actually spoke first. "That might be my fault," she said.

Declan turned his gaze on her. His mother was still beautiful and looked what she was, fifty-five years old, well-cared for, rich…

"Your father married me because I was respectable. I married him because he was not. It was my one rebellion in life. But we only married on the understanding that he would go legitimate and put his bad ways behind him. Your father was not a good man."

"Still isn't," Declan muttered.

"But I was determined you were not going to be the same. So you were brought up to know your duty, and you were a good boy. Better than we could have asked for."

"Are we going to get to the point?" Declan asked. Jess would be here soon, and he wanted answers first. Wanted to know how to move forward and his mother wasn't telling him anything he didn't already know.

"The point is, we went too far. You were too good. You were the perfect son, never a foot wrong."

"Except the summer you were eighteen," his father put in.

Jess.

"And after that you were even worse. Always perfect."

"I wasn't that bad," Declan muttered.

"Baby brother," Logan put in, "you're a goddamned machine."

Declan ignored the comment, and his mother continued, "I thought when you became engaged to Penny, things would be better, but in fact they were worse. She was just another symptom. I was glad when you split up. I told your father he had to do something."

"Something?"

"Shake you up, bring you back to life. Come on, Declan, tell me, are you happy? Have you ever been happy?"

"Once." He swallowed his drink, leaned forward, and poured another. He glanced up at his father. "So employing Jess was just your way of stirring things up. Stirring me up."

He shrugged. "If I'm honest, I'd given up. You were the perfect businessman. Hard to remember you were my son. But you got no pleasure from it. And I had no clue how to reach you. By the time you took that bullet I was willing to try anything. Jesus, I stood across from you in that hospital, you'd just been shot, and all you could think of was getting to some bloody meeting on time."

It appeared that Jess wasn't the only one to see through him, after all. He hadn't realized his family had felt like this about him. Had he really been so bad? "So you interfered? Again."

"When her name came up on the file, I couldn't believe it. Didn't at first—I presumed it had to be someone else. You know she has a medal for gallantry under fire."

No he hadn't. The report hadn't mentioned that.

"She's a goddamn hero. I would have put her down as a model or an actress. God, she was a beauty before that scar."

He gritted his teeth. "She's still a beauty."

"I am so looking forward to meeting this woman," Logan said.

Declan leaned forward, glared at his brother. "Keep the hell away from her."

"Not a chance in hell, baby brother."

"So, yes," Rory said. "I thought she might stir things up a little. Bring you back to life." His gaze dropped down over Declan, and his lips twitched. "And looking at you now, I'm guessing she succeeded."

"But what for? Why bother?"

"Because you're my son and I love you."

The thing was, Declan didn't doubt it. He sprawled back in his chair and scrutinized his father. "Well, I hope you're not anticipating a happy ever after here because according to Jess, that's never going to happen." He nodded at the check that lay on the table between them. "She had that framed on her bedroom wall."

Rory grinned. "You know, I actually like her."

"I don't think the feeling is mutual. And pity you didn't realize that ten years ago."

"Oh, I realized it, but it would never have worked back then. You were both too young and whatever you say—that girl had issues."

"Yeah, and you really helped with those."

"I'm not a fucking social worker. And it will all work out in the end."

"Love will find a way," Logan added, amusement clear in his voice.

"Jesus." Declan raked a hand through his hair. His family thought he was a fucking goddamned robot. And a miserable, un-fun-loving bastard. And they were no doubt right. After Jess, he'd stopped fighting it, just accepted his role in life, hadn't cared enough to change anything.

He remembered Jess saying that they were still so different. That even if they overcame the most obvious obstacles there would always be that fundamental difference between them.

But he was going to show her she was wrong.

The phone rang on the desk, and Rory picked it up and listened. "That was Pete. The guests are arriving and your girlfriend has just turned up."

The three on the sofa all stood as one. "I can't remember when I last looked forward to a party quite so much," Logan murmured as he passed Declan.

"I'm so glad one of us is having fun."

He didn't move as they all exited leaving him alone with his father.

"You want me to talk to her?" he asked.

"Hell, no," Declan said.

"Just give me a moment and we'll go through together. I need to change my shirt, some asshole just broke my nose. And on my birthday."

Declan sat, sipping his drink, contemplating the evening ahead. If Jess had her way, this would be the last time he saw her.

So he had to make sure that she didn't get her own way. She was too used to it anyway. Perhaps he wasn't the only one who needed shaking up.

. . .

The memories swamped her.

After that first time, Rory McCabe had banned her from the club. But on nights when his father was absent, Declan would sneak her in and they'd dance and party until the early hours. Her doing her best to tempt him, drive him wild, see how far she could push him before he would surrender, drag her off to some quiet secret corner, and make love to her until she could think of nothing else.

Tonight, the club had been closed to outsiders; this was a private party, but the room was already filling. She peered around, looking for anyone she recognized, any sign of trouble. She spotted Declan's two guards for the night on either side of a black door at the far end of the room. She nodded briefly, then continued her survey of the room. Otherwise, the only person she recognized was Paul, Declan's assistant. Though there were a few people taking more than an interest in her. She ignored them.

Her muscles tensed as the door opened and she waited for Declan to appear.

Just one more night. That's all she had to get through. All through the long day, as she'd ignored Declan's calls, she'd done her best to paper over the cracks so she could hold it together just a little while longer.

Then afterward she would take herself off somewhere, let herself fall apart, and then start the painful process of putting herself back together again.

And all day, she'd been fighting the nagging doubts that she was being a coward. That if she turned her back on this, one day—maybe not straightaway, but eventually—she would regret it bitterly.

Declan loved her.

But she couldn't let that matter. Could she?

Declan didn't appear. In fact, she didn't recognize any of the people who exited the room. A tall, stunning older woman with blond hair and a dark purple dress. A younger woman who must be her daughter, their looks were so similar. And finally a man. For a brief second, she'd thought it was Declan. But only a second. Tall, with Declan's midnight hair and sharp cheekbones. She was guessing this was the brother he'd mentioned. There was nothing of the respectable businessman in this man. All in black, with the black ink of tattoos visible at his throat and arms, he radiated bad-boy menace. Was this what Declan would have turned out like if he'd walked away from the role expected off him? A shiver ran through her.

If this was Declan's brother, then she was guessing that the two women were his mother and sister. Wow. It was hard to think of Declan as having a mother.

The door had closed behind them and the small group stood just inside the room talking among themselves. A third woman joined them. She recognized Penny, dark hair perfectly cut in a bob, makeup subdued but also perfect, and a stunning floor-length black gown. She obviously knew the family well. They chatted for a moment, then all four started searching the room.

Jess stepped back, mingling with the guests. The crowd was a mix of ages and types. Rory McCabe had an eclectic mix of friends. But if any were dodgy, they'd made an effort to hide it. She spotted Harry, a blonde on his arm, and waggled her fingers in his direction. The room reeked of affluence and respectability. All the same, she felt a twinge of unease, almost as though someone was watching her. This was the ideal setup if anyone wanted to get at Declan. Everyone would know he was here tonight. The place was a warren of dark corners where an assassin could hide.

She'd discussed all this with the team and with Rory, but he'd assured her that no one would get past his security, and in the end they had let the night go ahead. Now she couldn't help but think that was a mistake.

The light was dim and she turned slowly taking everything in, analyzing it in her mind, looking for any discordant note, anyone who didn't fit in. But could see nothing.

Her gaze kept straying back to Declan's brother, the one exception to the affluent and respectable description. The resemblance to Declan was uncanny. He'd separated from the little group and stood alone, leaning against the wall, arms folded across his chest as he watched the people around him. He radiated a faint sense of menace, like a panther who'd gatecrashed the party. As if sensing her gaze, he raised his head, and his eyes met hers, silver like Declan's.

He pushed off from the wall and strolled over, the guests parting for him. She'd thought his hair was short, but it was pulled back into a ponytail at his nape. He came to a halt in front of her and held out his hand. Black-and-red tattoos snaked down over his wrist and across the back of his hand. She took it in hers and watched his face. As she tried to pull away, his grip tightened.

"Jessica, I presume?"

"You do? You can drop my hand now. I'm quite capable of holding it up on my own."

His lips twitched, but he released his grip and her hand fell to her side. She resisted the urge to wipe it down her pant leg.

"So you're Jessica Bauer. Declan's unsuitable youthful indiscretion."

She raised an eyebrow. "And you're Logan McCabe. Declan's unrespectable black-sheep brother."

He grinned. "I like the description." His gaze dropped to wander over her body. It was weird; they looked so alike, but her body responded to Declan's gaze like a touch. With this man, she felt nothing. "I can't believe we never got to meet all those years ago."

"I believe you were a little indisposed."

"Shit, yeah. I was in the clink at the time." He studied her. "You know, you and I would make a much better team. Declan's way too stuffy for a woman like you."

"You know nothing about me."

"I've heard enough."

She couldn't begin to imagine. "And I've had my fill of the McCabe men, thank you."

"Oh well. It was worth a try to rile baby brother up a little."

"Do you do that often?"

"Whenever I get the opportunity. He was an insufferable little brat growing up. Always perfect, never in trouble."

"Unlike yourself."

"Yeah. At least come and meet the rest of the family. They are dying of curiosity."

"Really?" She wasn't sure she was up to satisfying that curiosity, but she followed him anyway. She found the whole idea of Declan's family unsettling. Maybe because she had demonized him for so long.

The little group opened as they approached. The three women watched her with cool expressions. She was guessing however curious they were, they were all far too well bred to make it obvious.

"Jessica, this is my step mama, Judith McCabe, my sister, Tamara, and"—he paused, a smile flickering at the corners of his mouth—"Penny, Declan's ex-fiancé."

Jess had been studying Declan's mother, now her gaze flashed to the younger woman, and she pursed her lips. "I hear you dumped him. Good move."

Logan choked back a laugh, but Penny merely smiled serenely.

"Ms. Bauer." Declan's mother stepped forward and held out her hand.

She so didn't need this right now. Why hadn't she made some sort of excuse and run away and avoided the whole fiasco?

Because she couldn't resist one last look at him.

Where the hell was he anyway?

She realized Declan's mother had been standing arm

outstretched for long seconds and she reached out and shook it briefly. What was she supposed to say—nice to meet you?

It wasn't. This woman was responsible for what Declan was today. And as far as Jess was concerned, she'd done a crap job.

"It's wonderful to meet you," Declan's mother said graciously. "I do hope we'll be seeing a lot more of you in the future."

She'd been staring at the black door; now she turned back, a frown drawing her brows together. "You do?"

"I'd like to think past differences can be forgotten and we can all move on. Be friends. I'm glad I've had this opportunity to welcome you to the family."

Had she stepped into some weird alternate universe?

"I'm not sure what Declan has told you, Mrs. McCabe, but I assure you I have no intention of becoming a member of your family."

"Call me Judith," the woman said. "And I'm sure Declan will clear up any misunderstandings you may have." She reached out and rested a hand on Jess's arm. Jess stared at it through narrowed eyes. She didn't want to call her Judith. She didn't want to call her anything. After tonight, she had no intention of being within talking distance to this woman again.

She wondered just how much Declan's mother knew of their "misunderstandings." And how the hell had a woman like this gotten mixed up with Rory McCabe?

And how the hell dare she welcome Jess to the family as though it was a possibility.

It wasn't. She could never be part of this.

Even if she wanted to.

Which she didn't.

And in that moment, she hated Judith McCabe for even suggesting the idea. For putting it in her mind.

Beside her, Logan leaned in close and whispered in her ear. "You look like you want to shoot her right now."

She cast him a sideways glance. "Maybe. And I do have a gun." She forced a bright smile on her face. "Well, it was very nice to meet you all, but I'm working tonight, and now I really have to go and check the place out for bad guys."

She didn't wait for anyone to say anything else, just whirled around and stalked off across the room.

Welcome her to the family? Was the woman crazy?

"Never going to happen," she muttered.

"What's never going to happen?" an amused voice said from behind her. She glanced around, to find Logan still close by. As she opened her mouth to answer him, the black door opened and this time Declan stepped out.

"Holy shit."

Chapter Thirteen

For a moment the room faded, the sounds of the music and voices muting.

Tall, dark, and dangerous. This was the bad-boy Declan she'd only ever dreamed about.

Beside her Logan lowered his head. "You like?" he murmured. "You know, it's the general opinion in the family that this vast improvement in Declan's appearance is all for you."

"Really?" But she wasn't paying attention, every cell focused on Declan. From his sexily tousled midnight hair, to the dark stubble that shadowed his jawline, and lower… She swallowed. The business suit was a distant memory, replaced by black leather pants that hugged his hips and long legs, and a black T-shirt that stretched across his broad chest. Heat washed through her, settling low down in her belly.

She didn't like to think she was so shallow as to be effected by a mere change of clothes but… "Holy shit," she said again.

Besides, it wasn't so much that he'd changed his appearance, but the "why" behind it. What he was trying to convey? That maybe he could change? Maybe they both could.

Dark glasses covered his eyes, but he took them off and stared straight at her, his gaze catching and holding hers, and a flame shot between them.

For long seconds they stared at each other, and she couldn't look away.

She was a self-deluding idiot. If she left Declan now, she'd regret it from the moment she turned away. And probably for the rest of her life.

Could she face her fears, overcome them?

"I'll leave you two lovebirds alone," Logan said, but she hardly heard the words.

She swallowed, quite unable to move as Declan headed toward her. He even walked differently, with the smooth glide of a predator, and something dark and needy uncurled inside her. As he drew closer, she saw another change, and her breath caught in her throat. His right arm showed the red skin and black ink of a brand-new tattoo. That was more than a change of clothes. It was a declaration of… She wasn't sure, but she wanted to find out.

He halted in front of her, and his gaze searched her face. "Are you all right?" he asked.

"I don't know." She shook her head, forcing her brain to function. "I think I might be."

She needed to touch him, check he was real, run her hands over the smooth leather… But as she took a step closer, she became aware of a prickle of unease. It shivered down her spine and she looked around for the source. In the army she'd learned to listen to her hunches. But again, nothing seemed out of place. She found the bodyguards at the edge of the room, their attention fixed on Declan. Steve turned to her, gave a small thumbs-up. All was well. She was being paranoid.

Maybe they could leave now. Get away from this crowd. Talk.

Do a whole load of other things.

She turned her attention to Declan.

· · ·

She didn't look as though she'd gotten any more sleep last night than he had, with dark shadows under her eyes. But she was still the most beautiful woman he had ever seen. He grabbed two glasses of champagne from a passing waitress and handed her one.

She took it but didn't drink.

They were in the middle of the floor, and he could feel a multitude of eyes watching him. He wanted to take her away, but wasn't at all sure that that wouldn't signal the end of the night for her and she would vanish, never to be seen again. So instead, he placed a hand on her waist and steered her into a dark corner behind one of the pillars.

Then he took the glass from her hand, put it down along with his on a nearby table, and pressed her up against the pillar. She didn't push him away, and hope rose inside him. Cupping her face in his hands he slanted his mouth over hers, sliding his tongue between her lips, tasting her. He was already painfully hard, and he pressed his hips against her belly, felt her push back and moan softly in her throat.

Finally, after long minutes, he drew back from the kiss

and rested his forehead against hers. Her hands were under his T-shirt, around his waist, fingers digging into his skin.

Christ, he wished they were alone somewhere. He wanted to lose himself in her, bury himself deep inside. She was going to walk away.

He knew it, and a sense of powerlessness washed over him. He was unused to the feeling and had no clue how to combat it. He'd told himself that he would do whatever was right for Jess. He wouldn't push her. But how the hell was he supposed to let her go?

"How about we go get some fresh air?" he murmured against her skin. "I know of this great alley, just close by."

A smile flickered across her face, but then was gone. She shook her head. "We can't risk it. Too many people know your whereabouts tonight. We have to keep you in clear sight."

He took a deep breath. Perhaps it was time to come clean. "It doesn't matter."

She raised a brow. "I think I'll be the judge of that."

"No. Really. My father fixed the problem, used his old contacts to call them off."

Her eyes narrowed. "And this happened when?"

He gave a small shrug. "The morning before we met at the club for lunch."

She pursed her lips as she studied his face. "So all this"—she waved a hand toward his bodyguards—"was a waste of time. And money."

"Not entirely. There's still some doubt about who's responsible for the letter bomb…" Then he shrugged. "Actually, that was really nothing more than an excuse."

"An excuse for what?"

He took a deep breath. "To see you again."

He tried to read the emotions flashing across her face, but they were gone too quickly. Loosening her grip, she took a step back, then considered him, head cocked to one side. "Steve said you got drunk last night."

"Did he say anything else?"

"Just that you'd felt the need to hit something and he'd taken you to the gym." Her gaze wandered over him. "I like the new look."

"I couldn't think of any other way to show you I can change."

She nodded toward his tattoo. "Can I see it?"

He lifted his arm, and she trailed her fingers over the tender skin of his forearm. She peered closer to inspect it in the dim light and something flashed across her face. Sadness? Regret?

He wasn't sure, but nothing that boded well.

It was the design she'd chosen for him all those years ago, their names entwined, with bloodred roses. The skin was puffy around the edges, but it was still easy to read.

She sighed and stepped back and he had the feeling that it was too little, way too late. He'd hurt her too badly all those years ago, and now she wouldn't risk letting him close again.

"Jess, I just want you to know—"

"Shh." She reached out and rested a hand against his chest. "Don't ask for anything tonight. Let's just be together, not worry about the future."

And why would she say that if she believed they had a future. Well, if all he had was tonight, he wasn't wasting it in the company of a whole load of people, most of whom he had no feelings for at all.

"Let's go then. To my place." She looked a little skeptical.

"Come on, Jess, I have one more night to persuade you that we can make this work."

For a second he thought she wouldn't agree. Then she gave a brisk nod. "Let's get out of here."

As she turned away, she frowned and reached into her pocket, pulling out a cell phone. She listened for a few seconds, her eyes narrowing in concentration and then flicking to him. She took a step forward, rested her palm against his chest, and pushed him back into the shelter of the pillar, while her eyes scanned the room.

Steve and the other guard for the night appeared out of nowhere as she closed off the call and put the phone back in her pocket. "You've heard?" she asked Steve.

"Yes, we need to get him out of here."

Obviously, they'd discovered something, some danger, but what the hell could it be. He trusted his father—if he said the threat was fixed, it was fixed. But she'd learned something that she wasn't happy with. "What is it, Jess?" A prickle ran down his back. Then he remembered the letter bomb that had devastated his apartment. They wouldn't try anything like that here would they? Not with all these people...his family. "Tell me, goddammit."

"Jake just got some new information." She pressed a finger to her forehead. "Did your father tell you who was involved?"

"He said it was better I didn't know."

"So he didn't mention your assistant?"

A frown tugged at his face. "Paul?"

"Apparently the DNA from the letter bomb was a match."

That didn't make sense. He would have sworn Paul was loyal to his father if not to him. "So he was in on the money laundering all along?"

"Right now, we don't know. Jake's looking into it."

"Paul's here tonight."

"I know. I spotted him earlier, but I haven't seen him for a while. We have men searching the place and your father's people have also been instructed to keep an eye out for him. They'll find him."

She turned away and spoke briefly with Steve, then came back to him. "We're going to get you out of here. This place is too difficult to keep you safe. Not only that, but if anyone starts shooting in here, it could get very messy. So we're going to walk out of here."

"I don't think so."

"You'll be surrounded. There's no way he can reach you."

"You think I'm going to let you risk your life to keep me safe?"

Her brows drew together. "Of course you are. That's what we're here for. That's why you employed us." She stopped and stared at him, eyes narrowed. "Except you didn't, did you? You knew there would never be any danger."

He didn't bother to answer; the question had been purely rhetorical anyway. "I'll walk out of here so long as you are nowhere near. I'm not letting you take a bullet for me."

"This is not negotiable," she snapped.

"That's where you're wrong." He folded his arms, leaned back against the table behind him. He wasn't going anywhere until he was sure Jess was safe.

She stared at him for long minutes. Steve leaned in close. "We're wasting time, Jess." She gritted her teeth, but then shrugged, though her figure was tense. She pursed her lips, studied him, her gaze dropping to the tattoo on his arm. Then she gave a curt nod. "Okay. I'll head out first. You follow once I'm away."

"Good. I'll see you at my place."

She made to go past him, but hesitated, and wrapped her arms around his middle, laid her head against his chest. "Be careful and do what you're told." Then she was gone.

He kept his gaze fixed on her as she strode across the room, her hair a bright beacon in the dim light. As soon as she had disappeared through the far door, Steve nudged him in the side. "Okay, let's go. Just walk casual as though there's nothing wrong. The car's parked out back in the alley. We're going to head straight there."

The skin down his spine prickled as he stepped out into the room. He searched the balconies around the edges, the pillars that created dark corners like the one he'd kissed Jess in. There were so many places a shooter could hide. But it didn't make sense. They could never hope to shoot him in here and get away afterward. Maybe it was conceivable that Paul might be holding some grudge, but Declan couldn't believe he was suicidal or that he'd risk spending years in prison.

Beside him, Steve was talking into his phone.

"Have they found him?" Declan asked as he finished the call.

"No. And they've searched the whole building. But this place is a warren. Too many places to hide."

Maybe Paul believed he could shoot in the darkness and in the confusion no one would know where or who the bullet had come from. At least Jess was safe and away.

They were nearly out of the building now. Ahead of him, Steve pushed open the door and they were out into the relative quiet of the corridor.

"Let me go check everything is secure outside," Steve said. The door slammed behind them and Declan jumped, then turned to see his father and Logan.

"What the hell's happening?" His dad did not look happy. "They told me it was Paul."

"We don't know for sure yet."

"I'll fucking kill him."

That was the dad he remembered. "They're getting me out of here. I'll call you later. Enjoy the rest of the party."

Steve appeared in the doorway and beckoned for him to come forward. He followed him out into the alleyway. A black car was parked at the curb, the engine running, and next to the car stood Jess.

Why the hell wasn't she halfway to his place by now?

His heart rate kicked up a notch. The air was tense, imbued with a heavy sense of anticipation he could almost feel. The night was still and sounds of intermittent traffic drifted down from the main street. He wanted to scream at her to run, but there was nothing to run from. He was being irrational.

Besides she wasn't the one in danger. He was. She would be all right.

He forced his feet to head toward the car.

Something moved in the corner of his vision.

A figure stepped out from the shelter of a doorway, arm stretched out.

Steve was in front of him. The second bodyguard at his back. The man had a clear shot.

Everything seemed to shift in slow motion as though he moved through glue.

"Declan!"

Jess called out his name, but there was no time. He swung around, ready to dive, vaguely aware of Steve turning. A loud *bang*, then another and his body tensed, ready for the shots as something crashed into him, hurling him into the side of the car and then down to the concrete pavement.

More gunshots.

Then silence.

He blinked open his eyes. His view was blocked by a tall figure who stood over him, legs braced.

His second bodyguard.

A dead weight lay on top of him, and he felt the warm seep of blood against his chest.

"Jess!" He struggled to sit up, leaning his back against the car wheel, Jess cradled against his chest, her long blond hair spilling over his arm, and even in the dim light, he could see the spread of crimson across her white shirt.

Steve crouched down beside him, checked for a pulse and nodded. "Try not to move her," he said. "There's an ambulance on its way."

Declan held himself perfectly still and stared down into her face, the lashes shadows across her pale cheeks. "Don't you fucking dare die on me."

• • •

In those few seconds, everything changed. The whole world took on a dazzling clarity.

She loved him.

And she wasn't ready to lose him again.

He was hers. That was all that mattered.

She'd dived for him without conscious thought, felt the

sharp jolt as the first bullet caught her in the side just as she crashed into him. Then a second had hit her in the arm, whirling her around. They'd crashed into the car, then the ground, her head smashing against something solid and for a few seconds everything went dark.

When she came to, she could hear a voice. Declan speaking urgently. She tried to make sense of his words, but her brain was fuzzy. Rain started to fall and the drops landed on her skin. In the distance she could hear a siren getting closer.

She forced up heavy eyelids. She had no intention of dying on him. But just in case. She squeezed his arm.

He must have seen that she was conscious. His hand stroked her cheek and he stared down into her eyes. "What is it?"

"I just wanted to tell you I love you."

Chapter Fourteen

Oh God, she loved him.

She drifted in and out of consciousness on the way to the hospital, and she was aware that Declan never left her side. She didn't know how badly she was hurt. She'd taken a couple of bullets. The one in her arm shouldn't be a problem, but the first one…

She just wasn't sure, and she couldn't lift herself to investigate.

Once at the ER everything had moved too fast. Before she could tell anyone she was all right, the gas mask was on her face and she was being sucked under.

When she woke again, she was in a hospital bed, and the room was in semidarkness, though from the faint light filtering through the blinds, it was morning. Well, she'd made it through the night. She took stock. There was a dull ache in her arm, a sharper one in her side, but other than that she felt okay.

She rolled her head to the side. An IV drip was attached to her arm, and just beneath that, Declan sat slumped in an upright chair, long leather-clad legs stretched out in front of him. His eyes were closed, dark lashes resting on his cheeks.

He was so beautiful. Asleep, all the harsh lines were smoothed away and he looked almost like the boy she had fallen in love with all those years ago.

But he was no longer a boy. He was a man. And she still loved him.

In that moment of clarity, she had realized that it didn't matter that it was the most stupid, self-destructive emotion she could ever feel. It wasn't negotiable. It had always been there, pretty much from the moment she'd set eyes on him all those years ago. It had been hidden, buried beneath a mountain of hurt, but it had never gone away.

And Declan loved her.

He was willing to give them a chance. And she wasn't exactly a good bet. It took a brave man to be ready to take a chance on her.

She'd been trying to hold herself together, had papered over the cracks, and now, she relaxed and the paper holding her together dissolved into nothing, and the cracks widened and tore, leaving her broken all over again.

And for the first time, she accepted that it was inevitable.

It occurred to her then, that all those years ago, she had in fact mended all wrong. Like a limb that had been broken and badly set, she'd put herself back together again, but she'd never really functioned as a proper human being. She'd always been afraid to feel, to give any part of herself. To do that, those old mends had to be rebroken, so this time, she could heal properly.

Lying in the dim light she pieced herself back together, a little bit at a time, all the while keeping her gaze on the sleeping man. Her man. He'd told her he wanted to try. She did, too. She'd somehow fit into his world, if that was what he wanted. Though looking at him now, all bad-boy leather and tattoos, she suspected his world was about to change drastically.

She twisted a little and pain shot through her. She must have let out a gasp, because Declan's lashes flickered open and he came immediately upright in the chair. His gaze flashed to her face. "You're awake. Thank Christ. Are you okay, in pain?"

"A little."

He pressed a button beside her head. "Before they come, tell me again."

She knew what he meant. "I love you."

"Shit, when you said that and I thought…" He ran a hand through his hair. "That was the worst night of my life. Say it again."

"I love you."

He rose to his feet, pushed back the chair, and came to stand by the bed. Unfortunately, the side with the IV stand, and he kicked it with his foot.

"Christ, I need to hold you and I can't even get close." He took a deep breath. "There was so much blood." His expression hardened. "Why the hell were you even there? What the fuck happened to meeting me at my place?"

"I had this thought. It occurred to me that there was no way he would try the hit inside the club. He must have known that he'd never get out without being caught."

"And couldn't you have just called and told one of my babysitters that?"

"I did. But then I thought I'd better just keep an eye on things until you turned up, and then…"

"Yeah, I know what happened then. You took a bullet meant for me when I'd told you that was the last thing I wanted."

She grinned. "Two bullets."

The door opened at that moment and a doctor entered, together with a nurse, and behind them Kim and Dani, both carrying a big bunch of flowers and a couple of carrier bags.

Pushing past the doctor, they hurried across the room, coming to a halt beside her and opposite Declan. They took turns to lean down and kiss her very lightly on the cheek. "We couldn't wait any longer." Kim nodded toward Declan. "Your hot new bodyguard wouldn't let us stay. He wanted you all to himself. But we've been getting hourly updates in the waiting room and we took it in turns to go out goody shopping."

Jess peered into one of the bags. It appeared to contain black lacy underwear, chocolates, and a bottle of scotch.

"Thank you," she said.

Dani bit her lip. "We've only been given thirty seconds, but we just wanted to say we love you and don't ever do that again."

"I won't."

"We'll be back later," Kim said.

"That's if your bodyguard lets us."

They both squeezed her good arm and then headed for the door. Dani spoke to Declan. "Look after her."

"I will," Declan said, reluctantly stepping back so the doctor could get to her. He leaned against the wall, arms folded across his chest.

"Are you in any pain?" the doctor asked.

She pulled herself upright, wincing as a sharp pain shot through her side. Then settled back against the pillows. "A little."

He added something to the IV and seconds later the pain faded to nothing and she sighed. "Thank you."

She closed her eyes as the nurse moved around, peering at the bandages, taking her blood pressure.

"How bad is it?" she asked the doctor.

"Not so bad. Both wounds are clean and we stitched them up. The arm one was simple; the one in your side a little more problematic. You'll have an impressive scar, but the bullet missed any organs and went right through."

"So can I go home?" Her voice sounded pathetically hopeful, but she really hated hospitals. Both her previous stays had ended up with just about the worst periods of her life.

"No." The doctor and Declan spoke in unison.

"You lost a lot of blood," the doctor continued. "We need to replace that and make sure you're stable."

She pursed her lips, but decided to wait until she felt a bit stronger before she started arguing her case. The truth was, she did feel a little light-headed. She hadn't noticed while she was horizontal, but now she was sitting up her head was swimming. She gritted her teeth.

"Stop fighting it and relax," Declan said. "You're not going anywhere."

"Who's going to stop me?" But she said it just for effect and snuggled back into the pillows. The pain was gone. She wasn't dead. Declan loved her. Time to fight for her rights later. Now she just didn't feel up to it.

As the doctor straightened from his examination, a tap sounded on the door. More visitors.

"Okay. You're good for now," the doctor said. "Ring if you experience any change."

"Thank you."

As he opened the door she caught sight of her next visitor. She really wasn't up to this.

Rory McCabe strolled into the room, a huge bouquet of bloodred roses in one arm, a garment bag in the other. He placed the flowers on the table by her bed and stared down at her for a moment. Then lowered his head and kissed her on the cheek.

She resisted the urge to wipe her face; it was really too much effort.

"To what do I owe this pleasure?" she asked.

"I just came to thank you for saving my son's life."

"All part of the service." She peered at him a little closer. His nose appeared swollen. "Have you been in an accident yourself?"

He smirked. "I came into sudden contact with Declan's fist, last night."

Shock widened her eyes. She turned to Declan. "You hit him? Why?"

"Why the hell do you think? Because he's a bastard. And it's been a long time due."

"Thanks," Rory muttered. He took a deep breath. "Jessica, I owe you an apology."

"Yes." She waited and he frowned.

"Yes, well, I'm sorry. It was wrong of me to offer you money to leave my son alone. But I love my son and I believed you were wrong for him. I still believe if the two of you had stayed together back then that it would have been a disaster."

"Has anyone mentioned that you suck at apologizing," Declan murmured.

Rory cast him a black look. "It's a first, and I don't expect to repeat the experience anytime soon."

But she knew he was right; back then she'd been a mess. She wouldn't have been able to cope with the pressures of the relationship. Because she had no doubt there would have been immense pressure. A seventeen-year-old girl with a low boredom threshold and a penchant for trouble, and Declan busy at college. She would have been in a strange country, without any family for support. Her sister wasn't all that supportive when she was in the same country. On a different continent, Jess reckoned she would have just written her off.

Maybe they would have survived. Maybe not.

"Okay," she said.

"Okay what?" Rory looked wary.

"Okay, apology accepted."

"So you forgive me."

"No. Don't push your luck."

He laughed. "I like you, Jessica. You've grown up into an impressive woman."

"Thanks," she said drily. "Praise from Rory McCabe. My life is now complete."

He laughed again, then tossed the garment bag to Declan, who was still leaning against the wall.

"What's this?" he asked, catching it.

"A change of clothes." He sank into the seat Declan had been sleeping in earlier. "In case you don't get home before you're due in court."

Of course, she'd almost forgotten about the court case, and Declan could hardly turn up in leather pants and a bloodstained T-shirt. "So tell me about Paul? Why did he want Declan dead?"

Rory shrugged. "He didn't. Not really—it was just a means of getting at me."

"And why did he want to do that?" It was Declan who asked the question. "I thought he owed you big-time. You paid for him through college, looked after his mother."

"His father was a bouncer. He was killed in a fight working in one of my clubs. It seems his mother blamed me, and brought up Paul to blame me. I took his father, he takes my son."

"And was it your fault?" Jess asked.

He shrugged. "Maybe. But you do those jobs, you take the risk. Anyway, he's been waiting for a chance at his revenge ever since and Declan provided it when he got involved with the money-laundering operation."

"So the first attempt wasn't Paul."

"No, that was the real guys. I should have guessed there was something dodgy when they denied knowing about the letter bomb."

"Yeah, you should have."

He stood up. "Okay, I'll leave you two alone." He crossed the room, paused at the door, and a smile twitched the corners of his lips. "Your mother will be pleased." And he was gone.

Declan came around and perched on the edge of the bed, took her hand.

"So what happens next?" she asked.

"I don't know."

"I bet that's a new feeling for you."

"It is, and it's a good one. But you were right. I'm stepping down as CEO of McCabe Industries. I need to change my life. It's just that right now I don't know what I want. Except for you."

She slipped her hand into his and squeezed. "You have me. And maybe we can just spend some time deciding what you want."

"Won't you be busy with your promotion?"

She shook her head. "I told Jake I don't want the job."

"You don't?"

"The strain of being nice was killing me. He says I'm welcome to stay, but I don't know, maybe I need a change as well." Her parents had been charity workers, and she'd always harbored a secret dream that she could do something similar, give something back. Maybe it was something she could look into. Later.

He laughed. "So we'll be footloose and fancy free."

"The world will be our oyster."

"We can go anywhere, do anything. Travel. Hey, what about a world tour of the ten highest bungee jumps?"

She opened her mouth to say he'd be on his own, but smiled instead—maybe some of the nice had stuck. "I'll stand on the sidelines and cheer."

"Perhaps not, then. I wouldn't want to jump without you."

They were quiet for a few minutes. Jess closed her eyes and relaxed back. Ten years ago, it would never have worked between them. Now they had a second chance. Maybe together they could work out what sort of people they wanted to be. She was ready to try. She was drifting into sleep when he spoke again.

"Jess?"

Her eyes flicked open. "Hmm?"

"I know it's too soon. But one day, I would be truly honored if you would have my baby."

"Babies," she murmured and drifted into sleep. "Lots of babies."

Epilogue

It was done. He'd spent the last month handing over his position as CEO of McCabe Industries to his sister, Tamara. She was scarily competent; he was sure she would do a great job. And their father was on hand to help if needed. Logan had promised to look after Grunt, and there was nothing else to keep Declan here.

As the doors of McCabe Industries closed behind him, he turned back for one last look and caught sight of himself in the glass doors. The businessman was gone. Maybe not for good, but for now. Instead of a suit, he wore jeans and a leather jacket. Way more suitable for what was coming next.

Jess waited for him at the curb, standing beside the gleaming black-and-silver Harley. A belated birthday present, she'd told him. They were off to discover that whole new world.

Jess slid her hand into his. "Are you ready to go?"

"More than ready."

He swung his leg over the bike. Jess handed him his helmet, then climbed on behind him, sliding close and wrapping her arms around his waist. He switched on the engine, and the machine rumbled to life beneath them.

"Let's do this then."

And they were off.

The End

Acknowledgments

I'm just going to say one thank you this time—to Rob, my husband.

It's been a tough year for us both. I was diagnosed with breast cancer just before Christmas last year, and we've been dealing with the consequences in the months since. Through it all, Rob has been great. He's driven me around, held my hand, looked after my animals, told me continuously that it will all work out, and nagged at me to keep writing. I have no doubt that without him, this book would never have been written.

So a huge, huge thank you, Rob!

Love you always!

About the Author

Nina Croft grew up in the north of England. After training as an accountant, she spent four years working as a volunteer in Zambia, which left her with a love of the sun and a dislike of nine-to-five work. She then spent a number of years mixing travel (whenever possible) with work (whenever necessary) but has now settled down to a life of writing and picking almonds on a remote farm in the mountains of southern Spain.

Nina writes all types of romance, often mixed with elements of the paranormal and science fiction.
www.ninacroft.com

And if you'd like to have learn about new releases sign up for Nina's newsletter here:
http://eepurl.com/rZ5rz

Discover the Babysitting a Billionaire series...

LOSING CONTROL

OUT OF CONTROL

Also by Nina Croft...

BREAK OUT

DEADLY PURSUIT

DEATH DEFYING

TEMPORAL SHIFT

BLACKMAILED BY THE ITALIAN BILLIONAIRE

BITTERSWEET BLOOD

BITTERSWEET MAGIC

BITTERSWEET DARKNESS

OPERATION SAVING DANIEL

BETTING ON JULIA

LOVE KNOWS NO BOUNDS anthology

THE DESCARTES LEGACY

Printed in the USA
CPSIA information can be obtained
at www.ICGtesting.com
LVHW022306040224
770932LV00032B/237

9 781505 529845